Hot Kitchen Snow

Hot Kitchen Snow

SUSANNAH RICKARDS

CAMBRIDGE

PUBLISHED BY SALT PUBLISHING

14a High Street, Fulbourn, Cambridge CB21 5DH United Kingdom

© Susannah Rickards, 2010

Printed in Great Britain by the MPG Books Group, Bodmin and King's Lynn

Typeset in Bembo 12 / 13.5

ISBN 978 1 84471 798 9 paperback

1 3 5 7 9 8 6 4 2

to Simon

Contents

Beau de l'Air

ONE MORNING, AMONG his dad's bills and his mam's prize draw notifications, there was a letter for Euan. He stood in the sunny hallway, in his school shirt and underpants, and opened it. A black-edged card inside announced the funeral of a Tracey Marie Alleyn next day at 3pm, with refreshments afterwards at 27 Crewdson Drive, Collingwood Park. Underneath a message had been added by hand: *it would mean the world to us all if you could come.*

He examined the writing to see if he recognised it but he didn't. Boxy letters in blue biro, a style he associated with his nan, with elderly women who never ventured opinions. Nice touch. He was pretty certain there was no such person as Tracey Marie Alleyn. He'd never heard of her. This was some scam set up by Ritchie and Jason to scupper his first proper date with Helen. Euphoria had made him stupid. He should never have told them she'd agreed to go out with him.

'*Les Enfants du Paradis*. It's, like, a special screening,' he'd told her, 'at the Literary and Philosophical Society.' He hoped the name of the venue would impress her. It impressed him. But she just said, 'Yeah, I know the Lit and Phil. My dad lectures there sometimes.'

'It's got subtitles.'

'Mmm, that'll be fun.'

He never knew if she was taking the piss. She had this

way of looking at him the same way she looked at puppies wriggling on their backs in the park.

'OK,' she said. Then, like she was quoting from an American teen movie: 'Pick me up Tuesday, school gates, at four.'

In the kitchen his dad was up to his usual tricks, cutting all references to the Royals out of the morning paper so their smug arse faces wouldn't spoil his breakfast read. His mam was buttering toast for herself, but as soon as Euan walked in she offered it to him instead. She was too subservient. He'd tried telling her.

He still had the post in his hand. On the off-chance, he asked them: 'Do you know a family called Alleyn, Collingwood Park Estate?' His dad worked at the Leam's cigarette factory just past Collingwood Park. Maybe it was possible someone had got the name wrong and it was meant for him. Three of his dad's mates at Leam's had died of emphysema only last year. But his dad shook his head, saying, 'Yer gin-soaked old sow,' as he shredded the Queen Mum's gummy grin onto his growing pile of off-cuts.

'You coming to this Goth gig at the crematorium the morrow?' Euan asked Jason as they hiked the steep short-cut up the bluebell bank on the school side of the Dene.

'What?' said Jason.

'Cool invite, like it's for a funeral. Think it's a gig or summat?' He waved the invitation at Jason who took it and stared, shaking his head.

'Tracey Marie? Nah, never heard of her.'

Euan glanced at him. He could just picture Jason and Ritchie ambushing him from behind a gravestone, water-pistols loaded with Concorde wine, chanting, 'Suck-errr,' at him for standing Helen up over their phoney invite. But it didn't look like Jason was bluffing. Master of the deadpan voice he might be, but when Jason lied his eyes always squinted. They were straight now, concentrating on keeping his balance. The climb was making Jason wheeze. He preferred the bus, but Euan enjoyed forcing him to walk occasionally. Jason needed trimming.

Not Jay and Ritchie then, but something was up. As he was walking through the lower school, this gaggle of girls jostled past him and he heard them whispering, 'Euan' and, 'Tracey Marie'. They kept turning back to stare at him, giggling nervously, but when he called out, 'Oi, yous lot, come here! What you saying?' they scarpered. Then Don Bird, Head of Studies, caught Euan as he came out of assembly and whispered, 'A word in my office at twelve, Nielson. Good lad.' Bird was always a tad theatrical, but he'd looked at Euan with such concern, dipped his voice so gently and gravely that a lump had formed in Euan's chest. What had he done? What was wrong?

It was a pisser. He'd planned to meet Helen at lunchtime, so he could intervene if she tried to change her mind about their date tomorrow, but she'd be in orchestra practise by the time he got clear of Bird. He'd told her he wanted her to look over his latest essay on *L'Etranger*. God, he loved watching her read his stuff. Loved how she sprawled on her stomach on the school field, her breasts almost touching the pages he'd written, kicking her legs up in irritation when she disagreed with what he'd put, so her skirt worked its way above her knees. He loved how her hair fell over her face, glittering dark and giving off a smell of almonds and how, when he tried to nuzzle her, pretending he was just reading over her shoulder, she swatted him away like a fly. Like his ideas were too important, too absorbing to be distracted from. And then she'd attack those ideas one by one with her slow, assured voice. She liked a good intellectual slanging match. There weren't enough lasses with brains, but he'd found her. Helen pulling books off the shelves in her parents' cavernous house, in vigorous pursuit of some John Donne quote, was the image he sent himself to sleep with every night, and he'd decided months ago he was going to glue himself to her till she got bored of fending him off and said yes. Part of him even sort of loved that she made him wait, though he'd had to keep convincing himself she was keen underneath, that she'd give in soon. And now she had. But he'd not get to Helen this lunchtime. Don Bird's summons sat like a cold pebble in his stomach all morning, making him wonder.

Another weird thing . . . At break, he'd been on prefect duty by the first form bogs, hustling out the smokers, confiscating their tabs, lamenting that the little tossers smoked Regal because they were cheap, not decent, filchable tabs like Silk Cut or B&H, when he'd noticed this dwarfy kid lounging against the radiator at the far end of the corridor, staring and staring at him.

'Oi, outside you,' Euan had said, which the kid ignored. Instead he approached Euan furtively and when he was no more than a foot away he blurted out like an accusation: 'You're Euan Nielson. Fucking be there, all right?'—his face filling up with colour at his own audacity—then fled.

Euan had never set eyes on the kid before, but he noticed the homemade black armband tacked to the sleeve of his blazer.

Don Bird kept him waiting twenty minutes. The bell for second sitting at lunch was just sounding as Bird appeared in his doorway with the school secretary and two sulking history teachers. 'Nightmare curriculum,' Bird was placating them. 'If I could choose between being dragged over broken glass by a galloping donkey or timetabling European Studies, I'd favour the donkey every time . . . Ah, yes.' He focused suddenly on Euan as the teachers mooched off. 'Patricia Alleyn rang and asked permission for you to be excused lessons tomorrow. Of course, of course, under the circumstances, you must go, and, er, Helen, no doubt will take impeccable notes in your absence. So sorry to hear about Tammy Marie.'

'Tracey Marie.'

'Yes, of course.'

But who is she? Euan was about to ask when Bird's phone rang.

'Bugger, bugger — excuse me,' said Bird, loping over to it, hand over the mouthpiece as he picked it up to add for Euan's benefit, 'Actual derivation, Bulgarian heretic, so not half as satisfying an expletive as one might wish. Who the bugger am I talking to? Oh, Headmaster, hello.' With a wink, Euan was dismissed.

So next afternoon at three he was not an hour away from an evening alone in Helen's company, but on his way to the crematorium with his hair gelled back and his school uniform on, because his mam had said just cos it was technically all black didn't mean he could consider for one minute wearing what he'd come downstairs wearing. She'd made him an armband and he'd borrowed the black tie his dad had got for the emphysema spate last year. He couldn't tell his parents he didn't know the girl. He didn't want their musings and phone-arounds. He just said he'd been asked to represent the school and they'd looked proud.

He'd never been to a funeral before. No one he'd ever known had died. This was still true. His dad had looked up where the crematorium was on the map, and Euan took the bus up the coast road that skirted Collingwood

Park. He knew the estate a bit. A couple of years ago he'd gone back there late at night quite often, to the houses of friends of friends, after Leams Factory Under 16s discos, before Iggy Pop and The Clash, before Helen, when he was still into Northern Soul. The houses were tiny and posh, oppressively clean and full of rules. Shoes off in the storm porch, no smoking, coasters under your coffee cups. But there was always a Jack Russell who clamped your leg and pumped himself against it, as if the dark desires these houses suppressed could be ejected through their small pets.

Had Tracey Marie figured on one of those evenings? Was she the sister of one of those lads? Had he snogged her once at Leams and forgotten?

The bus dropped him right outside the gates, but the cemetery driveway went on forever. In the distance, crowds were already thinning under the concrete colonnade of the crematorium entrance, heading inside. He was late. He broke into a jog. The sun was strong. His black shoes soaked it up, making his feet feel tight inside, and the heat itched his skin under his blazer, but he reckoned he'd best not take it off. A couple of lads his age were planting up flowerbeds in T-shirts and long shorts. Just for a moment he wished he could join them.

The chapel was packed. In a tiny anteroom off to the left, a coffin stood on a blue velvet plinth. In front of it four girls in his school's uniform, but much younger; second, third years, maybe, were sliding nasally through an a cappella version of an old chart hit:

'*Come show me your kindness*
In your arms I know I'll find it
Oh Lord don't you know with you
I'm born again . . .'

He slipped in the back, shirt wet to his skin under

his blazer, trying to take silent, shallow breaths, but his chest was tight from running and he couldn't stop himself gasping. A couple of heads turned and nodded sympathetically. A tissue was passed down the row to him.

'It is always difficult to accept the Lord's claim on our loved ones, never more so when they are taken from us in their prime,' the vicar began, as the four girls keeled back up the aisle to their row, clutching at each other, their cheeks striped blue with mascara.

'We want to shake our fists at Him and shout, *Why*? But it is not for us to dwell on why the Lord has chosen to recall Tracey Marie to his fold. Let us instead celebrate the life she had here on Earth. And what a full one it was. I don't believe I've ever seen this chapel so packed. To each of us here, Tracey Marie was special, remarkable. She has left an indelible, joyous impression upon us all.'

Rows of heads in front of Euan nodded, sniffed, let out choked chuckles of agreement.

He learned a couple of things from the vicar's eulogy. Tracey Marie had been a pupil at his school. She'd died of leukaemia last week at the age of thirteen, after a long, brave battle. He tried to conjure a picture of her in his head, some thin girl with purpled eye sockets, thought perhaps he'd seen someone around like that. Then the curtain was closing in front of the coffin and the chapel's PA system was whacking out Elton John's 'Song For Guy'.

It was 3:45. He should be in double French Lit now, with a direct view onto the netball courts where Helen had been playing in centre forward position for the past half hour. Perhaps if he slipped out now, was lucky with buses, he could get to the school gates in time and surprise her. He'd not even had a chance to speak to her to cancel—just left a message on her parents' answer machine.

He half stood to go, but saw that the family was beginning a formal exit from the front pews. Barrel-shaped women, crippled at the waist by grief; sober-suited men, their hands comforting and steering the shoulders of their wives, headed up the aisle towards him. Behind them, head so bowed his neck looked stretched for execution, was the minute kid who'd confronted Euan in the corridor the day before. The brother, then. His eyes flicked from side to side as he walked. They landed on Euan and his brows raised slightly, as if to say, 'You're here. Good on you.' As the family drew level with Euan, Tracey Marie's brother tapped the woman in front of him and said, 'Mam?' pointing him out to her.

'Euan, pet?' Her eyes were round and red. She looked like a guinea pig. 'You'll come back to ours?'

At the Alleyns, everyone knew who he was.

'Euan, lad. You can handle a beer?'

Too composed to be the father, must be an uncle. The man handed Euan a can of Tennants. Another man with the same gently sagging jowls, his skin grey, stood stiff-backed at Tracey Marie's mam's side. That'd be the dad.

The air was high with furniture polish and the gassy smells of snacks being heated in the kitchen. Euan moved to the closed window. On the sill were formal portraits and enlarged snapshots of Tracey Marie. He was right. He'd definitely not seen her before. She was white as meringue, moon-faced. A fat kid. In the earlier pictures, her thin blonde hair was combed excruciatingly tightly into bobbled bunches that jutted above her ears, drawing attention to the unfortunate width of her features. In more recent ones, her head was covered: gypsy scarves that made her middle-aged, a floppy velvet hat with a drooping rose. If he ever had a kid this happened to, he'd get her to show her baldness, not coddle the world from it with these desperate disguises. But in every photograph she was grinning. Real grins, not put on for the camera. He noticed the spots of light bang centre in her pupils. And in these later pictures her skin, though bloated with chemo, had a sheen to it.

Some relative bustled up to him bearing a tray. The hot scotch egg and pork pie smells were too much. He bolted away from her into the hall. The four girls who'd sung were sitting on the stairs, arms wreathed around each other, sniffling, sucking at cans of Panda Cola through straws. They gawped as he came through. 'Eeh, looka - it's him,' one of them whispered. He had to climb past them: he wanted the bog. Four pairs of eyes swivelled to his progress, like a hydra. One teen beast of mourning.

'Can yous shift?' He sounded gruffer than he meant to. His calves brushed their narrow shoulders as he passed.

What must have been the bathroom door was locked. The adjacent door had two tiles glued to it, the kind you get from Whitley Bay gift shops, printed with flowers and names: *Tracey* and underneath, *Marie*. He pushed it open. The room inside rushed at him. The rosy flush of the wallpaper, the duvet cover and curtains seemed to tint the air pink. A gang of pastel fur toys picketed the bed. A vanity table was crammed with lace mats, perfume bottles, red and mauve plastic love-heart photo-frames. He'd never seen anything so asphyxiatingly feminine. Girlie bedrooms. God, he was seventeen and he'd never been in a real one like this. He'd sat around in Helen's room sometimes, along with Jason and Helen's mates,

9

but hers was crammed with books and sheet music, with wooden masks on the walls: more studenty than girlish. And he'd never courted any other lass long enough to get invited back, just snogs on the Leams dance floor, on doorsteps, at bus stops.

A familiar, incongruous object caught his eye. On a painted school desk under the window, on top of a stack of *Jackie* magazines, was a Bantam dual language Baudelaire. Unlike his own copy, this was immaculate, the spine still shiny. It had barely been opened. Beside it was a stack of the dead girl's school exercise books. Looked like she decorated them. The top one was covered in felt pen. Over and over, in deft bubble lettering, she had graffitied every inch of the cover with his name.

Right down his body, his skin turned cold then hot. He pushed the top book so it overhung the pile. The one beneath was emblazoned with him too, this time in lightning zigzags. And the one below that with tiny lettering that spiralled out in a continuous flow: *EuanEuan 'meEuanNielsonTraceyMarieNeilsonEuan'n'TraceyMarieNeilson4eva'n'eva.*

He went to the vanity table. About half the framed photos were of him. Out of focus, long distance shots of him on the school playing field; him and Ritchie on their way to school, heads down, tabs to their mouths so they looked like a cover shot for some band; his head, the size of a pea, cut in a neat disc from what must have been the expensive group portrait of the lower sixth. Under the protective glass tabletop, between two doilies, was a pristine copy of the page from the local paper that featured him when he won the junior division of Newcastle University's French translation prize. It stared up at him. He remembered at the time a self-consciousness creeping in under his happiness at getting the prize, because the photographer had forced him to strike a stupid pose. When the item had come out, he'd examined the shot briefly, critically, and then forgotten it. But in this bedroom, it looked cocky, capable of more than Euan really was.

What had she seen in him? How could she covet that lank hair, that beaky nose? Why, as he now saw she had, had she traced the photo onto fine paper, and blocked in the panels of light and shade with contrasting inks, to make a Warhol icon of his face? There were several attempts in different colour ways, neatly tucked against the mirror. She'd labelled each one: *Euan in green and gold*; *Euan, reds*; *Euan, a study in monochrome*. The one she must've thought best, she'd framed: *Euan in purples and blues*. It endowed him with a louche, Jim Morrison edginess.

Who did she think of when she thought she thought of him? He needed to know. He searched the room now, swiftly, methodically, his heart quickening as he uncovered a padded diary with a flimsy sweetheart lock, easily snapped, and a scrapbook. He took them to her bed, with the few photos of herself she'd bothered framing. He shoved the cuddly toys onto the floor, took off his shoes and blazer, loosened his dad's tie. He skimmed the pages of the diary first, searching only for his name.

Today I told Miss Darrick I've changed me mind. I want to do French not Spanish. Euan does French A level. Je t'aime means I love him.

. . . Gold star day. Saw Euan. On a Saturday! Lord Jesus I thank you. You shine on me. I was in Jean Genie's on Percy Street and he went into Thorne's bookshop right opposite! I made Lisette follow me. We left Donna on the floor, screaming we'd promised to help yank up the zip on her jeans. I stood Right Behind Him, honest to God. He wanted this book called Bo der Lair. It's French. They didn't have it. Lisette said after it means something like ★Lover in the Sky★ (That is so dead

beautiful.) She does French already, lucky sow. But back to Euan in Thorne's. He was wearing his denim jacket and his dead faded Wranglers. I nearly died. And then Omigod when he turned around He Saw Me! He Looked Right at Me and He Smiled.

He read right through, every mention. One entry cross-referred him to the scrapbook. She'd been hanging round his house when he was out. *It's georgeous*, she wrote. *It's all covered in tiny stones. I picked some off the walls so now I have a Bit of Castle Euan in My Room!* She'd actually sello-taped tiny bits of pebble-dashing from his house into the book. A couple of the stones were still there.

Had a row with dad. He won't have the house done with pebbles. He says we're not a seaside B&B. I called him a cheeky pig. I heard him telling me mam the new drugs were making me nowty.

He felt gorged when he was done. He went back again and slowed down, reading some of the bits between. Hospital visits were perfunctory entries. There was scarcely any self-pity. The most he got was when her mother had bought her a teddy bear to cheer her up because she felt so dire after a vicious round of chemo. She seemed uninterested in her sickness, unthreatened by the brevity of her future. She wanted a life like Euan's, with Euan. She wanted to run her hands though his long, tangled hair, she said. She'd even learned a verse of Baudelaire translated by him for the University Prize. Not the caustic sombre stuff he usually favoured. She'd homed in on *L'Elevation*:

Beyond the boredom and the endless cures / that burden our fogged existence

Happy is the one who with vigorous wing / flies up into fields of light and serenity

Gutsy lass, he found himself thinking, searching for some of her racier bits to reread. She wasn't ashamed of anything she wanted. She'd only reached thirteen, but she'd put: *I'd do anything with that Euan. And I mean Any-thing. Honest to God. Upstairs Inside. The lot.*

And there was another long section devoted to the top button of his skin-tight cords and what might be under-neath. This little lass, writing all that because of him. Thinking, well, as *lads* do. He never knew girls could think that way. He looked at her photos again, at her plump white child's flesh, her benign bald head. Tried to imagine it, taking the blouse off her. How willing she said she'd be. How it might be nice, after all, to have all that marshmallowy flesh, those doughy half-grown breasts wanting him, joining in, instead of Helen's lean, restless, rejecting body. His stomach flickered. He rolled onto his front on her eiderdown and breathed in. It held that body spray and sweat aroma of the girls from Leams, wonderful to him.

He was lying there, holding the best photo of her, the one that showed her as far down as the waist, when her dad walked in.

'Son?'

Euan looked up. His face burned so hard he felt fever-ish, headachy.

Mr Alleyn came and sat on the bed at his side, bringing into her room the stale car smell that middle-aged men emit. Euan's own dad had it.

'You divvent need to get up,' he said. 'It's all right son. I understand.'

But Euan sat up a bit, cupping his hand over the broken clasp of her diary. He'd been lying there, talking away at Tracey Marie in his head, he realised. Mr Alleyn had interrupted them. The things he needed to tell her so crowded his mind that he blurted them out to Mr Alleyn instead: 'She's dead good at art. It's a bit tidy like, but it's gutsy, you know?'

Mr Alleyn nodded.

'Her writing's too neat, though.' God that came out shite. He glanced at Mr Alleyn, but he was facing away from Euan, staring out into her pink room. 'What I mean, like, some people are so stupid they reckon if you write that neatly, you haven't got a brain. Tracey, she had a brain.'

Mr Alleyn didn't reply. He suddenly buckled where he sat, and exhaled noisily. *Shit,* thought Euan, but then Mr Alleyn righted himself, with a pale blue rabbit in his hand from the heap Euan had ousted. He put it on the bed. Stooping and straightening, sighing with each exertion, Mr Alleyn reinstated her toys one by one. Euan shifted off the bed to give him room. He came and knelt at Mr Alleyn's feet to help, passing the animals to him. When they were done, he straightened up and hovered in front of Mr Alleyn. It was impossible to leave the room. He swallowed.

'Em, actually sir, I didn't know her at all.'

Mr Alleyn looked up at him. There were flecks of white skin in the bags under his eyes.

'Aye son, I know.' He reached for Euan's hand and held it, squeezing intermittently, rubbing Euan's palm with his thumb. 'I know that feeling very well.'

Mango

THE DAY BEGAN, as days did, with her father's voice, deep and perpetual, like a Hoover being dragged across the floor above. His rumble set Elsie in motion. Before she had time to caution herself, her legs carried her to her parents' room and into his fray.

Her mother lay in bed. Her father had stripped off his sleeping shorts and stood naked on tiptoe, viewing himself in the broken mantel-mirror.

'Hives. All over. Jan! *Jan*! It's those new sheets. I'm allergic. God, I need this. Didn't sleep a wink. I can't believe you didn't wash them first. You'll have to take them back. My audition's today. You knew that, Jan. You should . . .'

And on. Elsie tuned to the plock-plock of rain in buckets around the room. A chunk of ceiling plaster lay like an iceberg on the carpet. It had come down a few nights ago and landed on her parents' bed while they slept. Lucky it wasn't the head end, that's what they said. Her dad had pushed the bed into the dormer window where it was now. The light was better there, anyway. She hopped onto it—a momentary island—then climbed in at the foot. The new bedclothes were harsh and vinegary, her dad wasn't wrong, but the quilt cover painted her skin with shadows. She tunnelled against the limp warmth of her mother's cotton nightie, emerging beside her head.

'I love *my* new sheets,' Elsie whispered.

Her father was onto Tranter, the theatre's new direc-
tor. There were two schools of thought on acting, Elsie
knew. Tranter's fuddy-duddy Russian, and Daddy's
physical theatre. Schools of Thought; she imagined them
perched on twin clouds in a summer sky, with roads like
kite-ribbons trailing from them. The Russian school had
an onion dome, which Elsie secretly admired, but was
dingy inside. The actors went round groaning a lot and
clutching their stomachs. The physical theatre had red and
yellow walls, and people boinged everywhere as if their
feet had springs.

Her father had returned to his hives and audition. Her
mother sighed softly; just Elsie could hear. 'I was trying
to cheer the place up,' she said.

'If you want a 'nice life', screw an accountant and
move to Darras Hall.'

'I didn't mean that. And Elsie —'

'Elsie, nothing. Don't get at me. I'm the one red-raw.'

'I'm sorry, Miles.'

Elsie pressed her hands to her ears. She hated her
mother apologising. She did it often and for all the wrong
reasons. Her mother stroked Elsie's cheek and lifted the
hem of the curtain above her head.

'Must be going on twenty-to-eight,' she said, staring
at the rain clouds. Elsie was proud of her mother's ability
to tell the time by looking at the sky. A necessary trick:
they had no clock.

'Turn on the radio,' Elsie begged. If the DJ agreed
with her mother on cue, 'Twenty-to-eight and here's the
Commodores,' Elsie would shriek, thrilled by her mother's magicianship.

'That radio's knackered,' her dad said. 'Someone's
fiddled with it. I thought I'd banned it from the bathroom. Someone . . .'

'I'll stick the kettle on,' said her mother. Elsie sat up to join her, but her mother pressed her back into the bed. 'Stay here. Keep Daddy company.'

This was another of her mother's tricks, passing the baton sneakily to Elsie, who always fell for it. Now she was on duty to listen and soothe. As soon as her mother was gone he switched tack.

'She does it on purpose, you know,' he said, melodious with self-pity.

Elsie mimicked this tone when friends tried to fall out with her. It worked well, used sparingly.

'She knows my audition's today. She's a pretty little saboteur. If I was still single, Christ . . .' He yelped a laugh. 'Aguardo's over from Chile to co-direct. Tranter knows he's my God. This audition is crucial.'

'I thought it was for a horse in *Equus*,' Elsie said. She couldn't resist the probe.

Recently, when she spied on her parents from the stairs, this audition was all they talked about. Whether he'd be allowed to play a horse called Nugget or just a horse without any name, and whether there'd be a transfer, which wasn't a paper tattoo for your arm but acting in London for squillions. Her father had exploded when her mother asked why he wasn't up for the lead.

'I'm not a sodding teenager, that's why.'

'You've always played down.'

'Not any more, woman, look at me. Too old for juves, no gravitas for character. I thought thirty was supposed to be the moratorium for bloody actresses, not men.'

He turned now from the mirror, hoisted his jeans from the chair, pushing his legs into them as if they required taming.

'*Equus* is about a horse, Else. If I get Nugget I'm, in effect, the title role. *Equus* is . . .'

'Latin for horse, I know,' she said. 'It's in our Green Reader.'

She padded across the gritty carpet and patted him on the back.

'You'll be a good horse, Daddy. I like playing horsey with you. You're brilliant at it.'

'Christ, Else,' he said, 'I won't be plonking round the set on all fours, is that what you think? Where's your mother keep the calamine lotion?'

'She doesn't keep it anywhere,' said Elsie, 'but I know where it is.'

'Fetch it and put some on my back, would you, while I obliterate these grotesqueries.'

He swiped the sheets from the bed, exposing stained mattress-ticking.

∿

Miles had gone for his run. He'd be in Jesmond Dene now, Jan reckoned, limbering up on the flat rocks by the yellow-white foam of the waterfall. From there straight to the theatre, where he'd shower. He still felt a claim on the place from his time in rep before Tranter took over. Jan hoped the stage doorman would let him in.

The silence that fell on the house in his absences was textured, silken. Jan felt moved to sing. Elsie loved a good, mournful hymn: 'For Those in Peril On the Sea'. Or a folk song with tragic consequences. Jan began:

'Oh the briary bush
It bleeds my heart full sore.
If I once get out of the briary bush
I will never go there anymore.
Oh-oh, hangman stay thy hang . . .'

But Elsie didn't join in. She crouched by the gas fire,

claiming tummy-ache. A ruse. Jan had more sympathy for this pain than others. Sometimes Miles's wrath blew over her; her own patience and fortitude billowed against its gusts. But today it sat in her gut. Only the freedom of being alone in the house would release it. She'd send the child to school with one elbow hanging off, if she had to. She turned the toast under the grill and bent to Elsie, intending a brisk, 'Up and dress,' but the child was white-faced and sweating.

'Oh,' sighed Jan. 'Off to bed and stay there, then. I'll check on you when I'm done.' Which would be a good while. Elsie trailed away to her room. Her faded night-dress and scrawny limbs made Jan think of evacuees. She turned off the grill and scooped up the heaped sheets, hurled down the stairwell by Miles earlier, thudding past her in the hallway, as she'd been bringing his tea.

The sheets overfilled the twin-tub, but she crammed them in anyway. The very sight of them hurt. Jan wasn't one for purchases. She shopped only for food, in the covered market, at the day's end, when they were selling off. Bargains had made her an audacious cook: shark stew, oxtail goulash, coley in sorrel sauce. The fishmongers and butchers always asked, 'For the cat?' and she'd nod. Fools. Thriftily confident when it came to food, she was nervous of paying out for solid goods. Next-door handed her last season's outfits, and when Milly Partridge died, a host of practical items had come her way. Elsie had been horri-fied by her acquisition of Milly's housecoat, calling it a ghost's gown, but Jan fished it back out from the rubbish whenever Elsie tried to ditch it in there, and in the end the child gave up. There was no need for sentiment. Once word was out you took cast-offs, people were happy to oblige. She'd never yet needed new for Elsie.

The sheets were a departure. Her mother's hand-medowns were shredded with hedge-tears where Miles had thrust his heels through them, defending dream territory and she'd finally had to admit they were beyond repair.

Opposite the market was Brentford Nylons. Its lack of window display assured Jan she wouldn't be out of place. But the interior was a whirl. Ceiling banners unfurled promises of *Clearance Bed Linen* that *Must Go Today*. The colours amazed her. Sheets in turquoise, topaz, garnet. Covers that converted eiderdowns into instant continental quilts. Fitted corners. Matching pillowslips. Her arms filled of their own accord until she felt giddy. She parked her stash on a trough of negligees to examine the labels. 100% brushed nylon, drip-dry. Non-iron. So easy to care for! Recklessly she carried them all to the till.

Leaving the shop she felt glorious, as though the world were her chorus. Until now Miles had played supplier of frivolities, and she the staying hand. But recently his moods had all been sombre. In this small act of jewel-bright rebellion she'd shift roles. She'd blaze their bed with colour and prove her faith in his creed: when you're down to your last penny, blow a pound to remind the world to Provide More! She'd been so excited she tossed out the old linens. The new nylons were on the beds before Elsie returned from school.

Damn. The twin-tub was leaking again. Water pooled across the lino towards her bare feet.

'Mum? Mu-um.'

Elsie's weedy wail from upstairs. She'd do this first. She reached into the hot water for the sheets. They flared up and punched her. Punched right into the marrow of her bones. Punched so hard she was flung across the room and splatted against the china shelf. She slid down it, no muscles left to keep her bones upright. The veins in her wrist howled. The punch raced up her arm like a petrol flame. It kept punching.

Elsie appeared in the doorway. 'Mummy?'

Vital phrases skipped inside Jan's head. She couldn't marshal them into her mouth. What a sight she must be to the child: legs sprawled, head cocked at a loopy angle. The shocks began again, jerking Jan forward and back against the wall.

'Mum?' Elsie stepped barefoot into the kitchen, towards the flood of live water.

An image of that frail body tossed by the electric current brought heat to Jan's limbs. A fraction of control came back to them. Somewhere inside her, Miles's voice grew, booming to the back stalls: 'Elsie, don't move.'

'But . . .'

'Don't move.'

'Well, you get up.'

'I can't.' She had to find each word, position it in the sentence. 'Fetch Mrs Jeffrey, they have a phone. And put shoes on. Don't come any closer, d'you hear?'

Elsie was crying now.

'You need a cuddle, Mum. I want to cuddle you.'

'Get out. Get out of here. Stay out.'

Miles walked back from the Playhouse in the glittery rain, past the glossy lawns and drawing rooms of Brandling Park. The rain kept up the sweaty cling of his shirt from the warm-up. Tranter had barely used him in the group audition, he'd not even had the chance to balls it up. He'd tried a bit of subtle background work, but Tranter wasn't watching, it was obvious. That mousy, spectacled male, probably assistant stage management, clocked him and scribbled some earnest notes, but how much clout would he have? Life doesn't progress, as he once believed it would. It renders down, like the horse-hoof glue they use to size stage-flats.

The boutique windows on Clayton Road glowed in the gloom: Celeste's where, last birthday, he had bought Jan a spangled blouse for first nights and summer drinks.

'That'll drop off me,' Jan said when she opened it, holding it up against her apron. She'd talked *Celeste's* into a cash exchange and bought a length of poplin from the market to run herself up a couple of shifts when she had a moment. 'I need the day-to-day. That blouse was for once in a silly blue moon,' she'd confided in Elsie, knowing he was within earshot. The poplin was still folded in its bag, stuffed on the floor of the china cupboard.

He paused outside the expensive fruiterers next door to Celeste's, his eye caught by its display. Apple pyramids, pumpkins and baskets of huge green oval fruit, with a silvery sheen to their skin. Mangoes.

He hadn't tasted one since his Safari Shakespeare days, where he and Jan met, when they ate them daily for supper, their sweetness offset by the bitter insect repellent from their unwashed hands. Jan disapproved of the shop for its spiked prices, but their fruit was superior to the foamy, pock-marked apples she picked up on the market. Furtively, as if she'd caught him nipping into the betting shop, he pushed open the door. A bell tinkled overhead.

As Miles came out of the shop, a silver car hooted at him. Its driver pulled up to the kerb, beautifully cut hair swinging, pearl-painted fingers confident at the wheel. Leila Lewis, a local actress, up for the Equus role of the psychiatrist's friend, Hester.

'Hop in.'

He leaned in at the window. The car smelled of new

leather and Leila's jasminey perfume. If he'd married a woman like that, a bit older, born into a level of comfort she didn't know how to stray out of . . .

He shook his head. 'I prefer to walk.' Humiliating to be without a motor.

'Uh-uh,' Leila refused him, opening the passenger door. 'Picked up a message at the theatre. Your wife's unwell. I'll run you home.'

Jan unwell? His gut shunted queasily as he got in, bearer of rain stains to Leila's oyster-grey seats. The brown paper bag squatted on his lap.

'Who called? We don't have a phone.'

'Don't know. I'm sure she's OK. You should get a party line.'

He watched her slender, braceleted wrist, deft on the gear changes, as she pulled forward at the lights. Leila wrinkled her nose. 'Hey, what did you make of Signor Aguardo? Mucho low-key, don't you think?'

'Aguardo?' The queasiness surged to his throat. That bastard Tranter had kept them apart. Knowing they had so much in common . . . 'I didn't get to meet him.'

'Exactly. Just sat scribbling away like a clerk. The bespeccied one in the corner. Didn't you, twig? Had his eye on you though, eh? He told Alix in costume he wants you to make much more of Nugget than usual. Says the play's physicality needs more weight. Suppose Tranter's doing our psyche bits and Aguardo's doing your horsies. Nice mix, eh? And there's talk of a tour. Not for me, no thank you. Think I'll stick around for a juicy bit of telly, but, hey, that would be you sorted for a year, wouldn't it? Anyhow, here we are. In and attend to your wife. Send my love.'

∼

Elsie woke in the late afternoon. The sky was dark and her throat hurt. Springs from the bare mattress nipped her back and her nightie was drenched: she'd sweated out the fever. Where was her mother? They'd been put to bed together to rest, but that was hours ago, after Elsie had knocked for Mrs Jeffrey, who'd been calm and known exactly what to do, as if the event were planned on her calendar. She'd put her husband's gumboots on under her floral dress and brought a clean wooden spoon from her kitchen to turn their electrics off at the kitchen wall socket.

Then Mrs Jeffrey had thrown down cardboard packing to soak up the flood, and over it a pristine rubber-backed hearth mat from her own drawing room. It stood out, like a flag from a better country, against their floor. When the lay of the land was clear, as she put it, she coaxed Elsie's mum to her feet. 'My dear, sweet child,' she said, swaddling Elsie's mum in a blanket, 'you don't deserve all this.' Elsie liked Mrs Jeffrey's voice. It carried the soothing confidence of the minister at the Baptist Sunday School Elsie was allowed to attend sometimes so her parents could get their lie-in. But, 'Good grief,' Mrs Jeffrey said when she saw the state of her parents' attic, and she didn't smile when Elsie showed her the enchanted iceberg. She insisted they go back downstairs and tucked Elsie and her mum up together under a blanket on Elsie's unmade bed.

Below them, as they rested, Mrs Jeffrey hung the washing and made sweet tea. It didn't seem an ordeal for her like it was for Elsie's mum. It was all done in a jiffy. Then she went home to phone the theatre. Elsie studied her mother's face in the dim light. Her eyes were closed, her mouth was wide, her skin was softer than Elsie's. When she cared to, which was seldom, she looked beautiful. Elsie drifted but kept being woken by the violent jerking of her mother's body.

'Just shaking out the current,' her mum said, and next time: 'Just rattling my bones.' At last her mother slept and soon after Elsie did too.

The house was silent. Then came a soft laugh from downstairs. Elsie climbed out of bed. Her legs wobbled.

The kitchen was dark but for a column of hallway light shining onto the laundry pulley. The new sheets hung almost to the ground, a dim circus tent. Shapes shifted among them. She traced their movements to the floor, where four bare feet crisscrossed. Elsie drew back a sheet and stumbled in. Her parents stood entwined. 'My precious,' her dad was calling her mum. His face was wet. They turned and smiled at her and lifted her up between them. They'd been kissing and when they kissed her too, their lips were sweet and dripping from their own kisses. She pulled away. Her mother laughed.

'Oh Elsie, it's mango. Daddy is Nugget and he's bought us mangoes from the posh fruit shop on Clayton Road. Let's celebrate.'

Daddy held her as her mother play-fought through the sheets, returning with a broad grey-green stone and a penknife.

'Smell it.'

Elsie put her nose to the stone. Musty and squishy.

'Watch this,' said Daddy. 'Watch Mummy's trick. It's magic.' He felt through the sheets for the light switch. Sudden colour filtered down over them. Her mother sliced the stone across its centre. It dripped on the floor, the scented juice of their kisses. She drew some sharp lines in the stone.

'Watch her,' Daddy said. He was looking at her mother

as though she'd appeared from nowhere in a silver dress. Her mother cupped the stone with both hands, then, with a flick of her wrists, flipped it inside out. Gaudy quills of fruit stood up all over its dome. Her dad was applauding, his face striped in red and gold light. Her mother put the mango to Elsie's lips.

'Try it,' she said. Elsie tested it. The flesh sucked at her tongue, but after the prickliness it was sweet, reminding her she hadn't eaten all day. She bit into the mango, this grey-coated stone that her mother knew how to flip inside out, to reveal how good it could taste, how it glistened.

Hot Kitchen Snow

O NE HUNDRED LAMB shanks were simmering in three vats on two stoves in the galley kitchen of a cricket club; simmering for six hours, but still the flesh wouldn't fall clean from the bone, so Joy, that's the boss, told Richard, that's the new waiter, who until a month ago was fortunate enough to run his own company (like Joy), but became less fortunate than her when he ran it into the ground, hence his apron, black trousers and white polo shirt with the Bonne Bouche logo embroidered on its breast pocket —

told him to phone the butcher and have a go at him, because the shanks were frozen on arrival although she'd specified and paid for fresh and knows from her Leith training that a shank's unwillingness to turn tender in wine broth is determined by its freshness: frozen will never come good. The butcher had a go back at Richard and said the shanks were fresh when they left his shop and if they'd frozen since, it was the weather that was to blame, not him. It's true that outside the world was slowly being stopped by a weight of new snow,

which Joy had forgotten about in the heat of the kitchen, and because there were one hundred guests' appetites, stomach disorders and impressions of Bonne Bouche's effectiveness as a caterer to consider. Not to mention a culinary *coup de theatre* which was not Joy's thing at all, but which her client had insisted upon — a metre-wide apple tart to be flambéed at table which Joy was not happy about, given Health and Safety and the fact the only pan she had wide enough was normally used for paella so the heat might increase the smell of prawn she hadn't been able to eradicate. All this to consider, and pretty smartly, since the first guests were already arriving with snowfall in their hair like Christmas glitter, all stamping hoofish party shoes on the doormat, all exclaiming in surprise: 'Where's that snow come from?' as though there were other sources of snow than the sky.

Richard, dispatched now from the kitchen to collect coats and, bewilderingly, segregate them by gender into two cloakrooms, left and pink for ladies, right and green for men, never having played the part of cloakroom attendant before, felt barraged by the influx of guests, how they kept coming in and closing the door and ringing the bell and opening the door again, all stamping the same way and saying the same thing, smelling the same of strong musk and wet wool, which blend reached Richard's nostrils like the stench from cages of less lovable mammals at a zoo, the ones without humanoid properties of large eyes and fingerish claws. Add to this the pressure of every other waiter crying off because of snow, so Richard felt he should be simultaneously downstairs greeting and upstairs popping corks, and in the kitchen helping Joy, while all those coats kept piling into Richard's arms with no sense of his capacity to bear their weight and bulk, or see over them, which he could, just about, just enough to see clearly when

Dominic walked in

and as soon as he saw him, Richard realised that Dominic was the host and it was too late to do anything but smile and say, 'Can I take your coat, sir?'

Dominic's girlfriend, Allegra, came in behind him.

Richard saw her too. She was speaking to friends, saying, 'India? I totally don't see the point of going to India, since everyone else goes there and insists on telling one so very much about it,' as she handed her stole to Richard without seeing him, letting it land on top of the already over-heaped pile so its mohair pressed into Richard's nostrils confirming that it smelled only faintly of department store perfumeries and more strongly, as Richard knew it would, of the cage of a forgotten small mammal.

But Dominic saw Richard. Why, only six months ago, when Dominic first had the notion for a thirtieth bash, before he'd dreamed up the *coup de theatre* of a supersize *tarte flambée*, he'd roughed out a guest list and Richard was top. Dominic, who renamed everyone around him to convey their satellite function to him, had Richard pinned as his Main Man, and had been gutted, though he called it chilled, when Richard turned the invite down, and burning curious, though he called it delighted, when Richard gave his reason as a new job, but now, as he stepped in from the snow, Dominic's first thought was that his old mucker had shifted heaven to be with him on this night. He entered his party with an image in his head of Main Man Richard at a flight desk in some European airport, bartering with a stripling girl, insisting, part charm, part aggression, that she *had* to let him on an earlier plane, because his oldest friend and erstwhile business partner was turning thirty and he *had* to be there to see that birthday in.

'You're here! You deviant!' Dominic said. 'You told me you couldn't get out of working this weekend and here you are hosting your head off on my behalf, you sly dog.'

'No. I'm working,' said Richard whose voice and eyes

were steady, despite small patches of red spreading across
his throat as he transferred the weight of the coats into one
hand, just so he could press them down and puff out his
chest at Dominic, to draw his eye to the Bonne Bouche
insignia that proved he had packed in the company he'd
founded with Dominic to become

a waiter? At thirty? Not Richard, surely. Dominic
never met a man more hard-wired to succeed: up all night
on two phone lines and a Blackberry setting up Expec
with Dominic, snapping his fingers like a rap star at their
USP, spread-betting futures *online*. *Online*, man — punters
behave like online money isn't real. Call it online Poker
with shares and they'll sell you their children to be in. All
Expec had to do was get people to hear of them in the first
place, which admittedly involved stiff up-front layout, but
once people heard, once those kids were sold —

Except Richard binned it. Richard came in one
morning in a plain white shirt and black trousers, not
unlike the ones he was wearing tonight, and said he sensed
Expec had peaked and he wanted to sell before it crashed,
so Dominic laughed and Richard said actually he'd been
looking about for a buyer and there wasn't one, to which
Dominic said what the hell way is that to run business?
and when the fuck was he planning on developing the
decency to share such internal musings with his business
partner? and Richard said, look mate, he'd consulted his
soul, yes he really said that, so naturally Dominic made him
repeat it ten times in the diminishing hope that Richard
would realise what a nonce he sounded and crack a smile
and business would resume as usual, for loss of perspective
in a cracked man is a sad, sad thing to witness,

and now: 'I had no idea this was your party,' Richard
was saying. 'We don't get told the client's name. Just the
venue and hours.' His ears glowed red.

Dominic didn't blank him, he didn't ignore him; he turned away without replying only because at that moment he saw the stairs and a pair of good legs with silver spike heels disappearing up them into the cricket club bar, and remembered this was his party and he should be up there, not standing in a small and icy lobby blocking the entrance when there was a lackey here being handsomely paid to take coats and greet Dominic's guests.

Upstairs was cold and dim. It seemed they hadn't had time to locate the heating. When Richard returned to the kitchen from coat duty, Dominic overheard Joy asking him how it was out there and Richard correctly informing her it was cold and dim, and when she said she wasn't asking after the clients, ba-boom! Richard laughed.

Out of the hundred invited, Dominic had thirty guests show up. Thirty-one including himself. Should he count Richard? Thirty-two? Thirty-three including Medallion Knight, the Seventies DJ, but not including his ancillary staff member who never arrived because of the snow, turning out not to be that ancillary as he was the one with all the trad vinyl, whereas the DJ had only Donna Summer's disco version of 'MacArthur Park' to test sound levels, which he played and played with less apology than Dominic thought was strictly good for future business.

After Allegra finally spotted Richard on one of his canapé tours and cried, 'Richard!' and he replied, 'These are parmesan biscuits with goats cheese, sun-blush tomatoes and an olive, all home made,' he tried to go back into the kitchen, but she wouldn't let him. This was *Richard!* whose role it had been to have long desired her from afar, who commented daily on her hairstyle and fragrance, who called her a 'regular coat hanger,' and sighed perceptibly when he squeezed her a tad too long, sustaining Dominic's belief that she was still an asset, and Allegra's that she had an exit route should Dominic not work out

although Richard, his hands on her hips in greeting (bystanding guests: Is that Allegra, embracing a *waiter?*), discovered he no longer felt obliged to subtly *phwoar* her for Dominic's sake, that she felt to him tonight as she always had: as desirable as a ream of photocopier paper: her hips were similarly proportioned, similarly compact and hard-edged. He rocked her gently for a moment, but his mind was on work, on Joy at the kitchen door, chiming a wine glass with a fork, summoning the guests to dinner.

The shanks were served and sawn and pushed aside untouched and cleared away and in the dark the tart was brought to table. Richard wielded one side of the vast platter and Joy the other, then stood holding it while the guests chattered on, oblivious to the bloody weight of the thing, relittering the table Richard had cleared on the tart's behalf with glasses and bottles and useless belongings until Joy's voice sounded sharp as a bell: 'Excuse us, please,' which prompted the guests to dither and fluster and clear an ineptly small space. So Joy and Richard laid the tart down anyway, squashing the cigarette packs and silk stoles underneath, at which their owners emitted squeaked '*Oh*'s of dismay. As Joy turned to pour Calvados into a copper saucepan on a trolley by the table,

Dominic stood.

Joy's saucepan, heated by a nightlight burner, secreted two spoonfuls of dark sugar, for any chef knows the way to flame a pudding is to warm and sweeten the alcohol first, but Dominic, no chef, was up brandishing a bottle of *eau de vie* brought from home, loudly arguing its case over the caterer's Calvados to Joy who listened and said, 'You want to manage this?'

'Yes,' said Dominic, so she stepped back to let him slosh the *eau de vie* around the tart until all the guests warned what a flare there would be and scraped back their chairs to stand against the walls with gleeful alarm on their faces. Dominic flicked his lighter to the tart and stood well back. A small blue flame shivered and went out. Cries of *Ah!* He circled the tart and tried the other side, clicking his lighter until his own fingers were so scorched he had to abandon the project to the expert Joy who splashed a droplet of Calvados into the pan, heated it and the pan burst into flame. Cries of *Yay!* She tipped the pan and the flame flowed obediently onto the tart for her, rippling gold and purple for a pretty moment until it had warmed and ignited the *eau de vie* underneath. The *coup de theatre* erupted in an acrid bonfire of pastry and raw alcohol with a base note of prawn.

When it had been smothered with damp cloths, the fire door to the service balcony opened and the extractor fan turned full, Joy asked Dominic: 'Would you actually like us to serve this?'

Richard took one handle and Joy the other and the tart was carted away, as Allegra jumped up and insisted they play Virtual Record, whereby you request a song you really love from the DJ and he plays the disco remix of 'MacArthur Park' instead. By midnight, all the tables were pushed back and Allegra had show-ponied her way through 'MacArthur Park' versions of 'Sir Duke' and 'Tragedy' and 'SOS'. She had what guests there were all up and dancing.

Richard was no longer around when Dominic came to rest near the door to the kitchen which Joy had left propped open once dinner was over, as if there were an optimum time for show and once the night dwindles beyond it, the client may witness the hundred uneaten shanks he chose so carefully for his friends over a series of menu meetings and email exchanges some months earlier, being scraped into bright green refuse sacks.

This open door cast a wedge of yellow steam and light out onto his cold, dim, fucking party. He couldn't see Richard. Joy was in there scraping a plate and then with the hand holding the scraping fork, she wiped her hairline with the back of her forearm. She was the kind of woman Dominic would describe to friends as, 'A thoroughly decent bloke', but he was alone now; there was no one here with whom to judge her. He was free to savour how tall she was, how big boned, her thick hair tied back with the kind of red elastic band postmen drop on the pavement every few yards. She put down the fork and reached for an iron rod propped against the fridge, which she lifted to a skylight in the galley ceiling, prodding and prodding, her arm extended so her shirt stood proud of her flesh like a tunnel. Dominic could see right up it to the swirl of red gold hairs under her arms, which were a shock because women don't keep them these days, Allegra wouldn't. It might have been revulsion or desire, he didn't know, but something stirred him — oh — if he had stepped forward as he imagined himself doing, and pushed his thumb against her hipbone, her flesh would have sprung under his touch like good bread. And he might have, he would have, except

there was movement now in the dark recess beyond the fridge where Richard was sitting on an upturned beer crate, forking food quickly from a bowl into his mouth. He wiped his lips with the back of his hand, like a coda to her wiping her hairline with the back of her arm. Then he stood and walked into the lit kitchen and put down his bowl. Dominic could see from the smears left in it that Richard hadn't tackled one of the shanks. He had prepared himself a more palatable staff meal, or Joy had prepared it for him. Richard stood behind her, his thighs against the curve of her arse, lifted his arm to the rod, his hand over hers and gave it a shove. She gave it another and the skylight opened.

A column of snowflakes drifted down into the kitchen, switching about in the heat.

They both laughed and stepped back and, prompted perhaps by this snow, Richard pulled the fridge open. He took out a bottle of champagne he must have wittingly held back from the arrival drinks. He uncorked it now, pouring half the bottle into two water tumblers, which they drank from unceremoniously. They didn't raise a toast to each other or anyone, but drank it down as if it were water, quenching their casual thirst with Dominic's champagne, which Dominic wouldn't have resented—Richard would have been welcome to neck down magnums of the stuff—if he'd chosen to do it on the other side of the doorway.

Now Joy and Richard stood together under the snow, tipping their faces to it, pulling their shirts away from their bodies to let the flakes in to cool their skin. This, Dominic thought, this shaft of hot kitchen snow, was the *coup de theatre* he'd been after for his guests.

Allegra came reeling up to him in her silver dress like a whitebait and said, 'This one's 'Night Fever',' so Dominic called to Richard, 'This one's 'Saturday Night Fever',' and he replied, 'I thought I recognised it,' which made both the women laugh. When Joy touched Richard at the waist and pushed him forward, Dominic felt a heat in the same place on his own body. Richard took off his apron and came out onto Dominic's dance floor and shook his shanks to 'MacArthur Night Fever'. Having the waiter among them seemed to perk up the guests no end and they danced round him as though he were the highlight of the evening, clapping and whooping

as Dominic slipped away to sample the column of hot kitchen snow.

From the recess Joy said sharply, 'Staff only in here, please sir. Health and Safety.'

'Horseshit,' Dominic replied. 'This is fun.'

It was. It was extraordinary, like a wall of heat from the kitchen at his back and a blast of iced air at his front. Sensation Central.

'Everyone must have a go,' he announced. 'All my guests.' He turned to summon them and turned too far. The tiles were wet with snow and slick with lamb fat underfoot. They sent him skidding, and the hand he put out to the worktop to steady himself pitched a tray of champagne flutes into the air. There was a cheer from the dance floor as they hit the floor and some wit shouted, 'Sack the juggler!'

'Oops. Easy, tiger,' said Joy coming out of the recess with two bags of rubbish in her arms. Through the bright plastic he saw all that flesh, all those bones. On the floor, broken glass glittered beside the snow.

'Having a good time?' she asked, her brows steeply arched and when he said, 'Marvellous!' too loudly, her eyes stayed on his, making it clear that whether he was actually enjoying this palaver or lying, either way, he was the fool.

'I can do that.'

He reached for the rubbish bags, but she said, 'Please. Please go and have fun,' and headed past him to the fire door onto the service balcony, which she unlocked with her elbow and shoved open with her foot.

Dominic followed her out. Snow came at him from all sides, like it didn't know which way was down. He stood there in it, aware that Joy had moved straight back inside, that Richard was next to her now in the doorway, both watching him but talking of something else, of some garden party by a lake sometime in June, with hawthorn roses and wild strawberries, and Joy was asking, though it was far in advance, would Richard be up for it, did he think he'd be free?

'This is incredible,' Dominic tried to tell them, 'I can't even see my own hand in front of my face,' and Joy replied, 'I have to close that door now, sir. Would you please come back in?' as Allegra appeared in the kitchen doorway, beckoning Dominic, mouthing, 'People are leeeea-ving!' with faces crushing in around her, all calling, 'Goodbye. Goodbye-ee,' at which Richard held a finger up to them saying, 'Hold on, ladies, gents! I need to fetch your coats,' and up on the stage the DJ finally turned off 'MacArthur Park'. Joy ran the hot tap to wash the last glasses as Richard touched her back to say, 'About June; I'd love to, yes,' and Dominic paused before going back to his party to watch Joy whisk up the bright bubbles in the sink with one hand while the other clicked on the kitchen radio, so that at last, at last there was another piece of music in the air, and although it was only indifferent late-night piano, the change made it sound better than it was.

Guava Heads

I T'S MY FIRST DANCE. When I arrive at her house, Lauren takes one look at me and sends me in to her sister Zoë for what Zoë calls a refit and spray. Zoë sits on a white leather stool at a mirror framed in maribou and lights. She doesn't turn round when I come in but greets my reflection. I can see the long pale curve of her throat, her smoky eyes in the glass. I wonder what she can see.

'Sit,' she instructs. 'We'll potion you up after I've sorted out this shop of horrors.' She frowns at her immaculate face.

To me, Zoë has always appeared separated from the world by a sphere of something like golden light, if light had a transparent shell. I made the mistake of gushing this to Lauren once and she snitched to her sister immediately, but Zoë just said, 'Astute kid. I have a very large kinosphere.'

Zoë turns this way and that, her collarbones rising under her skin so gracefully I can't imagine how any boy at the dance could ever look anywhere else. For a moment I harbour some small hope that she can conjure a similar transformation for me. She studies my scrubbed cheeks, my floor-length blue, the band in my hair.

'Your mother's interpretation of dressy is beyond redemption,' she says.

She flings open the doors of her wardrobe and her clothes fly out at me, landing on the bed quivering.

Ripples of feather and angora, sequinned like tropical fish. I'm scared to pick them up in case I feel a pulse.

'Your first dance?' asks Zoë, stretching her outfits against me. 'You must sign the One Hundred Hour Pledge.' She picks up a padded book with a key swinging from it and taps it with her nail.

As she pulls a tiny angora top over my head, Zoë tells me not to give out in less than a hundred hours. She says that's how long it takes to know in your blood that the man's not a scrote. Her top barely covers my breasts. The silver threads running through the wool scratch my skin.

'A girl can't keep her brains in her guava, know what I'm saying?' she says. 'And guava head rules when you're out dancing. Heat of the beat, all that.'

When her mother calls her to the phone, I unlock the book but there's nothing to pry. She's only made one entry: a tick list of things a guy must do in the hundred hours he dates you before you give in. It automatically excludes any boy I've ever liked from school because he must take you for a country drive and spoil you rotten on a day trip to somewhere like Alton Towers. It includes a time-consuming, thoughtful and selfless gift, e.g. down-loading all your favourite R&B songs onto your iPhone in secret, even though he only listens to garage. I wonder if some of it's negotiable.

The Mayfair Ballroom is heaving. When I walk in beside Zoë, I expect the music to stop, the sea of people to part and light to fall from a mirror ball onto a spot where only she may stand. But hardly anyone looks up.

At the bar she says, 'What you tinies drinking?'

I ask for a half of shandy. She smiles and orders us all vodka and cokes.

'If he asks you to dance, take a look at your watch,' she

shouts into my ear. I wonder who she's referring to. 'If you say, 'Yes', the hundred hours has begun.'

A man comes and stands too close to me. He has a diamond in his ear and a leather jacket with a rip at the shoulder, showing off bare skin underneath. Although they're far too young to be let in here, I can hear the boys in my class hooting at him, 'What a tool! What a penis!' and rolling over their desks. They're still puppies. They don't have to do all this for years.

The tool puts his hand on my bottom. Zoë glides by and raises one gelled and mascara-ed brow. I step out of reach. He leans in and drapes his arm over my shoulder, though where his fingers dangle, it's not my shoulder anymore.

I pretend to be Zoë.

'Excuse me,' I say. 'I don't know who you think you're dealing with, but you'll be a long time waiting for any luck like that. I don't do anything for the first one hundred hours. I'm no guava head.'

The tool laughs. 'Is that a fact?' He looks too deeply at me, nodding slowly. 'Why not 99?'

'Sorry?'

'Why not 99 or 101?'

I can't answer.

'Is it because 100 is a nice, round number?'

The way he says it, round numbers sound really down and dirty. He comes and stands in front of me, so close his belt buckle scrapes my midriff. Zoë's angora crop-top makes me feel bundled up and undressed all at the same time. I think of my mother after school this afternoon, pressing the long panels of my abandoned blue, glancing over at me from time to time and beaming, and I wonder how she can be so seismically innocent at her age.

He lifts my chin with his finger.

'And what,' he says, 'is a guava head?'

I blush so hard it aches like sunburn.

'I don't know. It's Zoë's idea. She's the Hundred Hour Treaty queen.'

'The Hundred Hour Treaty queen, is she?' he asks. Now he's gripping my chin in his hand, letting me know he could crush the bone like an egg if he chose. 'Which one's Zoë?'

At that stage I still think that anyone who looks at her will see her golden kinosphere and know their place. When I point her out, I'm sure we are the victors. She's on the dance floor, sparkling like a prize.

He looks at her briefly then lets go of my chin and holds his hand out for me to shake. Because I can't think of anything cooler to do quickly enough, I take it.

'Your Hundred Hour Zoë needs to go back to school and check her sums. She's a notorious fatality in less than ten.'

He puts my hand to his lips and kisses it. His mouth is hot and wide and fleshy. His tongue nudges my fingers apart and slides in between them.

'See you around, Miss 99. Counting down,' he says.

The Dust Volcano

I T WAS TOUGH work digging under fierce sun, but
worth it. When Martin and Ghedi needed a break,
pairs of village men took over. If they flagged after a few
swings of the pickaxe, Martin joined them again, shovel-
ling vigorously. He was shoulder deep when the women
returned. They crossed the square barefoot, slender
ankles passing above him. Ghedi whistled and a tall girl
in indigo came over, a child wrapped to her back. 'My
wife, Atish,' he announced. She carried flagons of water
in each hand and one on her head.

'Thirsty?' she asked.

'Bring us beers,' Ghedi said.

Once a month, a lorry roared over the roadless scrub
bearing beer and Coke. The villagers' teeth were brown
stumps. Water was the luxury here. Each day the women
walked five miles to the river and five miles back with
heavy canisters. They were gone for hours. Martin's well
would change their lives.

The men stood in a circle, peering down. Overnight,
their hole had disappeared. After much conferring they
decided the culprit was a strong desert wind. They must
begin again. Ghedi stripped off his shirt and Martin put
one on. The skin across his shoulders was raw.

Atish came by on her way to the river, a basket of beers

on her head. She set it down, grinning shyly at Martin's loud appreciation.

'Get us some food,' Ghedi said.

Her friends loitered on the path until Atish returned with bread and boiled eggs, then they set off together in the heat, flicking their hands against the flies.

By sundown the hole was ten feet deep.

'Good work,' said Martin.

Next morning it was full again.

'Every shovelful we dig, two more cave in,' Martin said.

The men argued in Kiwaru and Ghedi summarised: 'Let's move the dug earth right away from the pit.'

They all dined together that night. Atish brought goat soup and beers. She lit a fire. The men sat chewing bitter leaves that numbed Martin's mouth and gave him churning, vivid dreams.

The following day the hole was fuller still, and their distant soil heaps had vanished.

'A geological anomaly,' was Martin's theory. 'Some underground turbulence is forcing the soil up. A dust volcano.'

But the men claimed the ground was possessed; they had disturbed sleeping spirits. Now they refused to work. They lay in the shade, drinking beer, chewing leaf and calling to the women as they passed to the river. Martin was wretched. He worked alone until the heat made him too giddy to continue. When the women returned, laden with babies, water, firewood, he braved them.

'We'll fight this,' he said. 'I'm determined you'll get your well.'

Ghedi translated. The women looked away impassively. They never met Martin's eye.

'Beer?' Ghedi offered.

Martin shook his head. He'd let them all down.

That evening he ate alone: sardines and crackers; rucksack rations. Afterwards he couldn't sleep. Perhaps he'd join Ghedi for that drink. By moonlight the village was bright as day, but monochrome. A grey goat hurtled towards him as he entered the square. He swerved to avoid it, and froze. Shrouded figures surrounded the well-hole, chanting to the percussive sound of soil refilling the hole. They worked in unison, no cajoling and breaks and discussions. Martin approached, grasped a shoulder. The digger's spade fell from its hand as it turned. Atish.

Martin sat with the women in the moonlit market place. Atish passed him the tea kettle and watched as he drank.

'We love walking,' she said. 'We talk some, sing some, nice and easy.'

'Oh.'

'If we have a well here, all day our men will shout: Bring beer! Bring food! Let's have a fire. Let's have — ' She rocked her body, nodding suggestively. The women held their bellies and laughed. 'No one asked us what we want.'

'I see,' said Martin. 'What now?'

'Do your work. Tomorrow. In the sun.' The women rose and resumed spading. Atish grinned at him. 'Or go and visit our beauty spots . . . The river is nice.'

The Last of Her

'JOSEPHINE? WELCOME. DELIGHTED to meet you. I'm Alice Gopal. Shower and a change, eh? And then I've organised tea on the lawn. Hope you're not too bushed. I've invited some girls round. Work at the British Council. Thought you might like to meet them.'

It could have been Surrey: rose carpets, freshly glossed skirtings, the neat blonde floss of Alice's hair. The cloak-room where Alice hung Jo's jacket was stacked with rare, familiar supplies: Kellogg's cornflakes, Persil, Robertson's jams.

Alice called through the house to her husband, 'She's driven all the way to Nairobi, almost from Somalia, in land cruisers and lorries, Raji. Isn't she adventurous?'

She smiled at Jo.

'Are you craving home cooking?'

'I've been living off *ugali* so long, I've forgotten.'

'How vile. Wallpaper paste. I've made you a colossal sticky chocolate thingy and some bread. Bread's appalling here, don't you find? I always make my own. Right now, we've snacks on the terrace and jugs of Margaritas for the brave.' Alice shimmied her hips stiffly. 'I'll show you up.'

She squeezed past Jo, patting a cupboard door. 'If you're feeling a bit travelly, washing machine in here. Bung it all in. Don't ask. Treat us like home. After you up the stairs, took a bit of a knock in the car the other day. Still slow on my feet.'

'How awful. Are you better now?'

'Mmm.' Alice dismissed the subject with a wave of her hand. 'Onward and upward,' she said.

Jo's bag, scuffed at the base, spilled patches of dry silt down the stair carpet, but if Alice noticed, she didn't show it.

'Had a super letter from Alisdair telling us all about you. He was your tutor at Kings?'

'Yes.'

'Very good. Well, we're delighted to have you.' Alice paused a moment on the landing, wheezing lightly.

'Voila!' she announced, opening a bedroom door onto chintz and pot pourri. Through a partition screen, Jo saw a sliver of pink basin and a gold mirror.

'Popped into town yesterday, picked those up for you.'

On the bed lay soap in pleated tissue paper, moisturiser, a Garrison Keillor paperback and a pack of tights.

'Apparently he's funny,' said Alice.

'Thank you. This is—you're so kind.'

Alice smiled. 'Not at all. We like our creature comforts here. You'll soon be in the swing. Come down whenever you're ready.'

She closed the door.

Jo unlaced her boots. Her body still whirred with the motion of the lorry. Her ribs were sore, her fingers burned and she couldn't stop her arms from shaking. She closed her eyes and the road out of Wakuru reeled past, its grey-gold scrub scattered with sections of unlaid pipeline from the abandoned water project. She could still see the piece of pipe that the village children had dragged onto the high ridge, the circle of sky gaping through it.

In the bathroom, Alice's taps gushed transparent water. The sound was shocking. Jo bowed over the bath to smell it. Good enough to drink, metallic and grassy, like in England. She undressed and lay on the bed, waiting for the tub to fill. Proper sheets. She put her face against them, breathed in the sherbet scent of washing powder. And then if she crooked her nose to her shoulder, the goat and cloves smell of Wakuru returned, coming from her own skin. Months ago, her sweat stopped smelling of her. She turned her nose from the pillow to her shoulder, back again. Wakuru, Nairobi-England. Now, lying on this bed, she was excited about eating English breakfast cereal, hot running water, tea without sugar brewed into it. She should stop feeling guilty. Coming to Nairobi was like going home. From the open window came the sounds of chinking glasses, someone squealing, a big splash and laughter. She got up to bathe. The dust she'd shed ghosted her image on the counterpane.

The Gopals were in the dining room when she went down. Alice had changed from her cerise tracksuit into a floral print. Raj was looking out through the French windows into his garden. He wore a yachting blazer and a turban of pale pink muslin. When he took Jo's hand to greet her, she thought she had never in her life met anyone so clean.

'The school here has two bells,' Raj informed her. 'One for break and luncheon and so forth, and one that warns there's a lion on the playing field.'

'Really?' asked Jo.

'Oh yes. It was rung last year.'

'Have you met Menace Minor?' asked Alice, scooping up a kitten from a cushion on the sofa. 'Raj says I'm Menace Major.' She twinkled at Jo. 'We found him along River Road. Scraping around in bins.'

'Not a lot going in the bins down River Road,' said Raj.

'And his fur,' Alice continued, 'all rotting away, falling out in clumps. Had to give you lots of horrid 'jections, didn't we? 'Normous vet's bill.'

The kitten bounded out of her arms and threw itself up the steps into the hallway. It had no hind legs.

'Couldn't walk at all when we found him,' said Alice. 'Shall we go into the garden?'

'I shall stay cool, if you don't mind,' said Raj, 'but ladies, have fun.' He smiled at Jo and kissed his wife.

The sun was strong. A table had been laid under a couple of fruit trees at the bottom of the garden which sloped down towards the Rift Valley. The Ngong hills stretched to either side. Two women were draped on sun-loungers near the pool. One was very thin with bright blue eyes, the other was yellow all over. Her hair was dyed blonde and her skin tanned to a pollen colour. A jug of iced Margaritas stood on the terrace between them. When they saw Alice they got to their feet and strolled over to the table, bringing the jug. Alice introduced the yellow woman as Charlotte Holland, the other as Hannah Blake.

'Have a Margarita,' said Alice, pushing a glass at Jo. 'Nobody wants tea right now. Or do you?'

'Margarita's fine,' said Jo.

A maid appeared with a tray of snacks. In her pink and white uniform she looked like a nurse. She handed round a bowl of crisps. They tasted sweet.

'They are *cassava*,' the maid told Jo.

Inside the house the telephone rang and Raj appeared on the terrace, beckoning his wife indoors.

'Tell them I'm busy, Raji,' Alice called.

But Raj mouthed something to her and she got up with a sigh and hobbled inside.

The two women pulled their chairs together out of the

shade and Jo was ignored. They talked of a tennis club and moaned about a man they knew who raced cars. Menace Minor came loping down the garden and hoisted himself up onto Jo's lap. She scratched his ears and he let out a rattling purr.

Wakuru was filled with black shapes and white moon-light, bright as day. A cow wandered past, its bony hind quarters poked up at the sky. Jo sat on the hut step having her last cigarette before sleep. She'd learned to smoke in Wakuru; it was a good taste, better than the food, and although it made your mouth dry, it kept insects at bay. Martin joined her. The moon made white discs of his glasses and the hairs of his beard stood out like black grass.

'The post arrived today,' he said. 'There's not a single volunteer app in it.' He tapped his beer bottle angling for Jo to speak first. His nails were like horn. She couldn't see the colour in this light, but they were thick and yellow when he gripped a spade.

That was the night she agreed to stay on after her place-ment ran out. She'd stay until the project was completed, however long it took. When her ticket back to Heathrow was two weeks out of date, she used it as a spill to light the lamps in the hut.

'What do you make of our view?' boomed Alice, coming back down the lawn.

'Stunning,' said Jo.

Something cut in front of the sun in the sky above them, and for a split second the garden turned hazy. Jo looked up. A large bird was circling their plot, so low she could see the pale feathers on its underbelly.

'Vulture,' said Charlotte, topping up her drink. 'Bloody

nuisance. They'll swoop right down and have the meat off your plate.'

'Watch out for Menace Minor,' smiled Hannah, 'they'd have him too.'

Jo needed to pee. She lifted Menace off her knees and stood up. Spines of white light hurtled towards her. She sat down again.

'Drink,' she apologised.

'Oh,' said Alice, 'are you dry? Top her up Hannah.'

The telephone rang again and Raj tapped at the French windows. Alice stood up with a sigh.

'Charlotte, Hannah, look after my guest.'

The women looked over at Jo.

'Are you going to buy a ticket for Alice's ball?' asked Charlotte.

'I don't know anything about it.'

'October 5th. Kenton club. Ever been there?'

'Not yet,' said Jo.

'Coup to have it there. Raj wangled it for her,' said Hannah.

'Good cause,' Charlotte continued. 'Alice's in all sorts of pressure groups. She's very involved.'

'She seems kind,' said Jo.

'Oh, she's barking. Fifty guineas. Good cause.'

'Are you dry, girls?' asked Alice, appearing with a fresh jug of cocktails.

'I'm being very good here, Alice,' said Charlotte, 'Trying to drum up trade for your ball. Haven't convinced her yet.'

'She'll have her sleeves rolled up, anyway. We're raising funds for the school,' Alice explained. 'All the money here's tied up in the Church, but they should have the choice, don't you think? Shouldn't say it, but I'm not very Goddy myself. Are you?'

'No,' said Jo.

'Oh good. Don't want to offend.'

In the distance the phone rang, stopped for a moment then rang again immediately, but no one inside picked it up. Raj rapped at the glass. Alice frowned and waved her hand at him in dismissal.

'Get rid of them.' Her voice carried well.

'They won't go.'

'Tell 'em it's Sunday. I've got guests, they've a bloody cheek.'

'I told them.'

'Hang up on them.'

'He'll call straight back. Harrison.'

'I know who it is,' Alice bristled. She topped up her drink and took it inside.

No one spoke for a while. Jo looked out at the land beyond the garden. The valley was broader and greener than any in England, and filled with a constant whistle of insects.

So many set backs: the baked ground, the shoddy tools, consignments of water pipes all different widths. All the money pouring in from the UK, squandered on back-handers and bribes to officials. There was nothing left. The villagers took the news without surprise. They drummed their desiccated goats up the main street and set them to graze on the powdery scrub, as they always had. 'We've had aid projects before,' Yinka the beer-seller said. 'They never last long.'

Everyone was leaving. Jo watched Leo stuffing T-shirts into his scarlet rucksack, debating whether to give his Swatch to a village boy. He was going back to Europe to help a friend run a hot air balloon company. She could just imagine him in a field beside some Loire chateau, waving to honeymooners, applying the same easy energy to releasing the balloon from its ropes as he had to attacking the baked ground with a pickaxe. Not seeing the difference.

Ross and Janine, the water project romance, were taking a final holiday before heading back to England to get married. Martin had given them the keys to his land cruiser. They were going to sell it for him when they got to Nairobi. He was headed for Tanzania. Kilimanjaro expedition. Something he'd always meant to do. Whenever Jo passed he seemed to be leaning up against the hut wall, stretching his hamstrings, tightening his thighs.

'How about you, Josie?' he asked.

'I thought I might stay on.'

'Here?' Leo choked on his beer.

'No.' Jo flushed. 'In Kenya, I mean. Find work.'

'Ha. She's smitten. She'll be selling up in England, shipping it all out.'

Let them think it. Let them never know she was stranded, with barely enough to get to Nairobi, let alone England, and certainly no wearily willing parent to wire money. Out of the question asking one of them for a loan. You can't borrow money unless you've already got it. She was desperate to go home.

'If anyone hears of anything fun going . . .' she said. She reached lazily for another bottle of Tusker.

Hannah reached over and grabbed Jo's wrist.

'Tell me about London,' she said.

'What do you want to know?'

'Everything. What are people wearing. What's opened? Shows, you know. And restaurants. Where are people buying? We get the *Times* here, days late. Bloody British Council. Especially what people are wearing.'

'I've been in Wakuru three months. I'm a little out of touch.'

'Don't care. My boss has had me out here two years. I'd kill for this month's *Vogue*.'

Ross and Janine had given her a lift as far as Lake Naivasha. Jo watched them drive off up the new road to the safari lodge. Chunky chalets, freshly whitewashed for the season, were dotted at careful random across the thick grass. The sickle lake glittered beyond. She got out her map. Kenya was the size of her palm, and the distance between Naivasha and Nairobi only as long as her thumb to the first joint. Ross had offered to drop her at the village, buses ran from there, but she was down to three Kenyan shillings. She turned in the opposite direction and set off along the unmade road that ran along beside the lake.

The ground was pale and pitted with holes the size of graves. One step was on solid ground, the next plunged her knee deep into a crater filled with floury soil. Within minutes she was shrouded. The dust forced its way in at her mouth and her eyes, worked into every opening of her clothes. She itched and burned. The man who'd directed Ross to the lodge had said: if you get to the chemical plant then you've gone too far. There were bound to be lorries going from there to Nairobi. She could hitch a lift.

Inside the house, Alice's voice was raised.

'No, I'm not listening. You mustn't call here again.'

When she returned her face was mottled. She sat with a thud between Hannah and Jo.

'Bloody ridiculous people.' She picked up a glass and put it down again, pushing it away.

'Might take a dip,' said Charlotte. She and Hannah rose simultaneously and crossed the lawn to the pool.

Alice's red face juddered. She sat back in her chair and spread her weight.

'Stupid bloody people. Won't let up.'

'Committee?' asked Jo.

'What?' Alice barked. 'No. This bloody accident.' She rubbed her hip. 'I was driving home down that dreadful road, no lighting you know, and this stupid woman steps out and gets herself clipped by my car. Didn't even know I'd touched something.' Alice glared at the hills. 'How was I supposed to know she was there? It was the middle of the night. They shouldn't be allowed on the road at night. They're not visible.'

Grey grids swam over Jo's eyeballs, with a surge of tequila and salt in her throat. She swallowed it back.

'These people, bloody Harrisons, driving behind me,' Alice was saying, 'took down my number, reported me to the police. They said I should have stopped. I'm hurt too, you know, car went spinning and my hip took a real knock. Try telling that to Harrison.'

The maid placed a fresh bowl of *cassava* crisps on the table. When she reached for Alice's glass, Alice smacked her hand away.

'You didn't, then?' Jo asked Alice.

'What?'

'Stop?'

'What? Course I didn't, didn't know she was there, did I? She was all right, anyway, the Harrisons took her to the hospital. Now they want me to go and visit her there. To apologise. She'll only ask me for money. You can't give these people money, you know. Can't start that. Now they've got hold of my number and they keep calling.'

The fatty smell of the crisps, the salt. Jo turned her head away.

'Couldn't you go? If you were in town anyway, I mean.'

'What? No. She wasn't seriously hurt. Tap on the head or something. Oh and the fuss she made, wailing and waving her legs.'

Menace Minor hurled himself up the back of Alice's chair on his muscley little forelegs. She let him clamber over her shoulder.

'They want to charge me, but we'll show them, won't we, Menace.' She lifted his stumps and let them fall onto her breasts. Lift, thud, lift, thud. The kitten dug his claws in deep and rattled loudly.

The wheels were five feet high. Jo climbed up using the hubcap and tyre treads as footholds, scrambled over the side and dropped into the well of the interior. The driver had offered her the cabin, but it was safer to keep her distance in the back, she thought, and more fun. She'd hitched on the back of a lorry in Greece once with a friend; miles of scalped countryside in the strong sun, with a good rush of wind in her hair. Like an advert for Coke. But the sides of this lorry were high, she couldn't see out. The driver pulled off and the lorry keeled steeply, spurting up dust as it hauled itself back onto the road. She pressed herself against the side. With her arms above her head, she could just about grip the rim with her outstretched hands. Couldn't keep it up for long, but the ride would get smoother soon, surely, and then she could sit.

She was sharing with a small load from the chemical plant: sheets of corrugated iron, red with corrosion, and reels of barbed wire. The driver hadn't bothered to strap them down: the sheet iron bounced and clanged against the metal floor with every bump, and the reels rocked as if gearing up to spin forward. The lorry lunged into a pit in the road sending her weightless into the air, soft as a doll, only the tips of her fingers in contact, then her knees were slammed hard against the lorry's side and she was back on the ground. The pile of sheet iron shunted towards her. She edged her way to the far corner, gripping as she went, like the sides of the swimming pool when she was a child. It was impossible to think. Her mind flashed with brief messages to her family, their exhausted, fretting faces, then fused and crackled white light, wouldn't land on a thought long enough to shape it. 'Oh, please,' and 'Oh, God,' poured out of her mouth as her body flapped. It was unbelievable how flimsy she was, unable to keep charge of her own flesh.

They hit a flat patch. She relaxed, dropped her arms for a moment; they burned from being raised for so long, but the lorry skidded and lurched in the dust and she was slammed across the floor. As she landed, a reel of barbed wire dislodged itself and thrashed into the corner where she'd been moments before. An empty Tusker bottle jangled after it. She tried pressing her body weight into the floor — better to lie flat if she could get some purchase — but the next plunge came and a sheet of iron sliced past her face. This was the last of her. This was it: this dark walled square of sky with dust pluming over it like sea spray. Then they were back on the flat and she was worming her way on her belly to the front, squeezed up against the shifting pile of corrugated roofing to hammer on the cab to be let out. She had no idea how far they'd gone, how long she'd been in there. She banged and screamed, but he kept on driving. If he had the radio on — and he was used to his load thumping around — her hand against the back of the cab would barely register.

There had to be a road soon, and traffic lights. She was longing for traffic lights, visualising them clearly, as Leo at suppertime in Wakuru had summoned up puddings and wine. They looked so good in her mind: a neat, narrow strip of road with a grass verge and the kerb painted white. New, clean traffic lights, the coloured filters gleaming, the lorry pulled up calmly at them. She could see the red glow. He'd have to stop sometime. There had to be a town soon, where she could vault back down. A twisted ankle, maybe, a hot dry walk, the bliss of simple discomfort. The desire for traffic lights was making her giddy.

She climbed up onto the stacked sheet iron, gripping the shiny front of the cab. The stack rocked like a surfboard. She buckled her knees, tried to relax into its sway. Just over the cab roof she made out a thin strip of grey green scrub, broken in the centre by a line of red. The dirt road had changed colour, they were away from the lake. They'd come onto a good patch, she might even be able to skirt round and get her bag before she jumped. She let go, the top sheet of iron skidded under her weight and slid off the pile.

She went down screaming. Her hands shot out to break her fall, landing on something warm and soft behind the iron roofing. She looked down. Maroon cloth and skin. A dark ankle and a yellow sock, a maroon suit jacket, buttoned tight. His arm was over his face, but she saw his eyes. The whites were flecked with amber. She reached out a hand to pull him up, but he just stared back at her, didn't lift a muscle to change his expression. She thought for a moment he was dead, felt the sticky shedding of fear across her back, then his lids rolled slowly over his eyes and a hand fished out from under the iron to scratch at his thigh.

They'd stopped. All this time she hadn't fallen over, they must have been still.

'Are you all right?'

The driver might not even know he was in there. The man groaned, not looking at her, twisted his neck as if testing it.

'Do you want to get out?' she shouted. But she was already backing away from him, scrabbling for her bag. 'Let's get out.' She was up, balanced on the tiny jut of a screw on the lorry wall. He closed his eyes. She dropped her bag down and jumped. The ground jarred her bones right up to the teeth. The lorry pulled away, churning up dust, pumping out scalding dark smoke.

Raj came out of the house and stood for a moment on the terrace, watching Hannah and Charlotte swim. He adjusted his blazer and the sun caught his buttons, then he sauntered across to Alice and Jo.

'I can see Alice is in good hands here,' he said, smiling at Jo. 'Ridiculous business.' He stroked his wife's knee with a clean, square hand. 'What the Harrisons don't realise is, it's all theatricals with these people. Nothing more. Harrisons haven't been here long. They're very naïve.' He surveyed his garden calmly.

The women were climbing out of the pool. They brushed the water from their thighs, shook back their hair and waved.

'Wonderful swim,' Hannah called to Jo. 'Aren't you on for one?'

Heat rippled across the water and the grass. Jo blinked, tried to steady herself, form a reply. Alice put her arm round Jo and called back, 'Plenty of time for that. She's with us now for the year, teaching at the Ken. Not as if the weather's going to break.'

The women laughed and nodded.

'I think I must—Excuse me,' said Jo.

After the brightness of the lawn, the dark house caved in around her. She rubbed her face. The maid appeared from the kitchen with a stack of white towels. Stairs first, Jo thought, pink toilet bowl, throw up, bed. Try not to get it in your hair. The spines of light came back with another surge of salt and lime in her throat. The white towels bobbed towards her through the gloom. Limbs flailing in the headlamps, the yellow palm twitching back under the iron after he'd scratched. She reached out for something to steady herself. The maid's arm was hard and dark like a banister.

'Terribly sorry. So sorry,' said Jo. 'I must've had too much sun.'

'Or drink.' The maid's voice was sonorous, precise.

Something blotted the light from the French windows. Alice had followed her into the room. She was at Jo's back saying, 'And it never rains here, except for the rainy season.' Jo aimed for the stairs and the sofa keeled like cattle on the main street in Wakuru, like a road. Here for a year. The floor lurched up and the ceiling swung down. She gripped tight to the maid's arm. Alice came round the other side, put her hand on Jo's back, releasing the smell of her underarm. It was like old coins.

'It's OK,' Jo struggled. 'I can manage. I can walk.'

The Margaritas rolled inside her like a storm. She lifted her leg, stuck out her foot. Somewhere underneath was solid ground.

Moon

WHEN MY SISTER was small she asked our father for the moon. Mine ball. Get it.

He stretched his hands out of the open window. It was a warm night in mid May.

Too far, he told her.

She bawled. She wouldn't let up. Her sobs fell like axes all night. No one slept.

Next evening I watched my dad hoist himself up the oak until its slender skyward boughs could barely hold him. The moon was low in the sky. He whacked it into the web of branches, where it struggled, palpitating, then locked it under his arm and brought it home.

In our room it banged against the ceiling, cream light churning with alarm as my sister poked it with a garden cane, commanding: 'Get down.'

We weren't the only ones who didn't sleep that night. The neighbours came out red-eyed and hoarse. The sun was up at midnight, they said. Madness. And it stayed up, double-shifting the sky for weeks. I watched it at times, in the small hours, its light greying under the strain.

By August my sister had tired of the moon. She weighted it to the floor with an old princess crown, then tossed her second blanket over it and it was forgotten.

I opened the window. My sister was downstairs. I took off its shroud and crown and carried the moon to the window. It twitched at the scented dusk air. In my hands it was cold and gelatinous, leaving a faint metallic smell. I tipped it onto the sill. It shuddered and wobbled unsteadily, afraid to rise. But the sun had spotted it and heaving with relief bowed out behind a rocky island. I scooped up the moon and lifted it high. It was heavy: my arms ached as I tossed it back into the sky.

Blizzards

I WAS IN THE garden with Helen. She had TOIL. That's what they called it at the organisation where she worked. Time Off In Lieu. Which means she prefers to work too hard, so sometimes they have to force her to stop by not allowing her into the office on a normal working day. That's Helen. I was using this aberration in our routine as an excuse not to tinker with my thesis.

I call it a garden. It's a scrap of yard, paved with York Stone-effect concrete slabs from B&Q, with white plastic loungers that the previous owners couldn't bring themselves to cart away when they sold us the flat.

'One day we'll get some decent garden furniture,' I said to her.

'Yes,' she said, 'and then the arguments will start. We'll look back on the old days fondly, when we had ugly handed-down deckchairs and still talked to each other.'

Actually I didn't want to let this comment go. I mean, what was she insinuating by that? But she was stroking my bare thigh (I was wearing shorts, it was hot) with the rough sole of her bare right foot, which was intensely physically distracting, and she was smiling at me sleepily through half-closed eyes, like a cat, so I just replied, 'OK, let's keep all our mad old furniture and stay happy. Deal?'

She rubbed higher up my thigh in response.

'When I was little,' she said, 'we had a country cottage we went to in the summer. I mean, it wasn't ours, we didn't have that sort of money, but we rented it from a friend of my dad's and we thought of it as ours. We left stuff there, from year to year. All the rickety stuff, like tin openers that were so blunt they'd have driven my mum mad if she had to rely on them everyday, but on holiday it was a sort of funny pleasure to struggle with a tin for a while. We used to climb over into the farmer's field and eat raw ears of wheat. I can remember how sweet they tasted. I still love worn out rose wallpaper and chairs that wobble. They make ordinary days into holidays. Did you have things like that?'

We are still at the 'Did you?' stage of our marriage, for which women appear to have an endless appetite.

Suddenly Helen pulled her foot from me and drew her legs up onto her own chair with an 'Oh!' I thought she'd seen a rat in the garden.

'The Aga,' she said suddenly. 'Oh, it was awful. I can't believe it.'

'What?'

'I'd forgotten. It was so awful I'd suppressed it . . .' She breathed in and out slowly, eyes closed.

'I used to love to light it. That was my ritual when we arrived at the cottage. You had to brush out the old cinders and stoke up a fire in the lower oven. Only this time our friends, the Lindhursts, had arrived a bit earlier than us at the cottage across the road and I wanted to play with Anna Lindhurst, so I just stuffed the coal and fire-lighters in, lit it, shut the door, and went to play with Anna. My mum must have been unpacking upstairs or something. Anyhow when I got back my mum and dad were standing in the kitchen and the smell from the Aga was evil. My mum refused to cook on it. In the end my dad opened the oven I'd lit and . . .'

She put her hands over her face but kept talking through her fingers.

'And my dad raked out—oh—a mother field mouse and her babies. She must have made a nest in there and I hadn't checked the oven because I was so excited about seeing Anna. I cooked them alive and that was the smell.'

She shook her head. Her hands had slid down from her eyes now, but still covered her mouth. 'I don't believe it. It was so awful. Have you, have you ever done something like that, something so awful, you can hardly bring it to mind?'

'Uh,' I said. 'Let me think.'

But then the phone rang inside the house and distracted me. I got up to answer it.

'To the best of my knowledge, I've always been perfect. That's why you married me. Right?'

'Get me a drink, would you, when you come back,' she said. 'It's getting hot already.'

I brought out two tall tumblers, packed with ice and fizzy water with a splash of lime cordial. When I was making them, it got me thinking, just a few months ago I'd never have dreamed of having this drink. It's Helen's drink. She has imposed it on me and explained its precise proportions. But I like it now. I would drink it even if I were on my own. Maybe.

'That was Jean-Luc on the phone,' I told her. 'He's coming to London. I said we'd put him up.'

'Jean-Luc?'

'Lucky Luke. I've mentioned him a thousand times. My old ski-mate. We were instructors together in Val d'Isere for years and years—right through college and when I started my PhD.'

'Oh,' said Helen. 'Maybe you've mentioned him. Before my time. He's back in touch? That's nice.'

'Yes. But I saw him recently. I told you.'

'You did?'

'That night in Engelberg.'

I'd done one last season in the Swiss ski resort to pay for our wedding, just before we got married. Helen hadn't wanted us to be apart, but the money was necessary. Still is.

'It was my last night and I had that cut-price flight home bang in the early hours. I'd waved off all my skeenies and was going to get an early night, then into the bar walks Jean-Luc. I've told you this story.'

'Don't think so.'

'Oh, well, I hadn't seen him for years. Couldn't believe he was in Engeldorf the same time as me. He's a riot. A real scamster. Signed us into the good restaurant at the hotel instead of the tour bus dive. Lobster bisque, Remy, all billed to our tour operators. Fantastic. I'll take you there, I promise.'

'For our Eventual Extended Honeymoon.' Helen smiled at me.

'Indeed. So . . . he'd left his wife, married his mistress, found a new mistress half his age, all very French. I showed him your photo and he was genuinely chuffed for me. Soft old heart, really. Anyhow, he suggested a game of chess. I hadn't played in years. We used to all the time. And he's quite good. Very wiley mind. So we went to the bar and played until it closed, but we couldn't stop, so we carried the set into the lobby. By now I was thinking there's no point in going to bed, my flight's at five. Luc got us two more lovely large ones from the bar and there's a knock on the door. The concierge is in his bed behind the desk. I can hear him snoring, so I opened it.

I'm almost knocked backwards by the snow driving in at me like armed police. So I'm shouldering the door to get it closed again and while I'm trying, in with the blizzard comes this man, blind drunk, in half a tux. Lost his jacket somewhere. Tie knotted round his forehead.

'Where's my wife?' he demands.

'Can't help you on that,' I say.

He stands rocking, frowning down at me.

'Havin' dinner. Very long dinner,' he explains, 'Then back to the bus like a little crocodile.' He toddles his fingers through the air. 'But I saw — most fantastic — watch! In a window. Top watch. Ever so detail. And they're gone! My wife — gone.' He splays his arms in wonderment.

'What hotel?' asked Jean-Luc.

'Hmmm!' goes the man, utterly challenged. After a time he announces, 'Got very pointy roof.'

'Oh, right. That totally narrows it down,' I tell him.

We help him back outside. The pavements are skating rinks. He skids, taking us with him, most of the way down the drive. We steer him in the direction of Engelberg-strasse – most hotels are on that run, and say goodnight.

We're so frozen when we get back that our fingers can't grip the chess pieces. Jean-Luc fixes us another brandy and we're just thawing, when the door's whacked open and, hello, it's our friend again. He weaves over to us and sits so heavily on the arm of my chair that it tilts, so he grabs me to break his fall and then stares at the chessboard.

'You bores?' he says. 'You pair grandpas, eh?'

'*Qu'a't'il dit?*' asks Jean-Luc.

'Should be out rousin', your age. Wouldn't catch me pussyin' round chess. Bloody *chess*.' He flings his arm dis-missively across the board, knocking the pieces flying.

This time we take him as far as the lower car park, but there's no sign of a coach still waiting for him. The air is so cold it ignites my teeth fillings, makes my kidneys ache. I feel old.

'Where's my wife?' the man cries. 'Val-rie!' Her name rings round the mountain. He lifts his arms like Harry Secombe, enjoying himself. 'Va-ler-rieeeeeee.' Lights go on in the chalets round the coach park. The snow's picked up speed, falling so swiftly now I can hardly see Jean-Luc on the other side of the man but I hear him say, '*Ta geule*,' and perhaps he gives him a nudge because the man keels backwards and lands, legs in the air.

We scarper. I've never been so cold. I had to think hard just to make my legs move. I had to send out orders to them. That's what happens when you technically freeze — it feels like your limbs are much further from your brain than usual. When we got back we didn't even speak. I just crawled to my room and sunk in a hot bath, topping it up until the room was thick with steam.'

'And the man?' Helen leaned in towards me. Her skin smelled hot.

Not over yet,' I said. 'No sooner am I dry and back downstairs than thudding starts on the front door. Jean-Luc gets up.

'Beyond the call of duty, my friend,' I say, but this time he just slides the bolt over the top and swings by the reception desk to put some music on, turns it up. I keep thinking the staff will come down or the guests will complain, but they've been skiing all day and they're dead to the world, so we light up a crafty Marlboro — the only one all season, I promise! And we set the board straight and played till dawn with that blizzard still ramming up against the windows. Unforgettable night. So.'

'So?' asked Helen. 'What does 'so' mean?'

'So . . . That's Jean-Luc. I thought you wanted to know.'

'That story's about Jean-Luc, is it?'

'That's my most recent Jean-Luc. There are others in my portfolio. All manner of wheezes and escapades, if they appeal.'

'How long have we been married?' Helen asked. She had her arms over her face to protect her skin from the sun.

'Three weeks, two days, twenty-one hours nineteen minutes and seven seconds.'

'I'm not sure I feel too good,' she said.

'That's because of where you're sat,' I told her. 'You're unprotected. The sun's moved over. It's right on top of you. You know you should get out of it, but I bet you won't.'

She sat with her eyes closed and her arms still crossed over her face, wrists exposed, like citizens in war zones when they come out in surrender. She didn't move at all, even though I'd warned her. Even though she knew she'd get burned.

Dog in the Yard

THEY ARRIVE SINGLE file. Tina's father leads the way like a scoutmaster, his arms out in an aeroplane to cool his underarm sweat. So embarrassing. Her mother follows him, moving methodically under the weight of her rucksack. They are abroad and Tina feels sick most of the time. She is stranded for the summer without her friends and the towns are full of churches with frescoes and you have to smile and say, '*Buona Sera*,' to strangers and be thankful all the time.

In the distance her father has paused under the shade of the youth hostel porch. He turns to herd his flock and seeing his younger daughter lagging at the gate, waves her to join them. Her mother waits a few yards away from him rubbing her shoulders. Her sister Cheryl has taken off her backpack. Tina can see from the way she's circling their parents that she's asking for a can of Coke. Tina's new trousers are stitched with nylon thread and the seams are rubbing her legs. She sets off at an elaborately slow pace. Maybe if she takes long enough there won't be a church this afternoon.

Half way along the path she stops outside a fenced-off yard where a ferocious dog is barking. She stands stock-still and waits for it to shut up, but it barks. The dog is tied to a post and screened from her by a stretch of chicken wire, but still she can't move past it. It lurches and stumbles towards her, caught in its tether.

She edges to the far side of the path and squashes up against a prickly pear bush, waiting for it to ease up, but it rears towards her, yowling and pawing the air. A sharp stone has worked its way under her jellybean sandal and is cutting into the little toe of her right foot. She won't let herself shake it out until she's past the dog, so she has to devise a routine that will allow her to move. Close your eyes and open them three times. Each time look at the dog and see something different about it. Whenever she's frightened of something, her mother makes her describe it. Sometimes it works.

Eyes scrunched, Tina breathes in.

Go. Its lolling tongue, the gums and goo. Her eyes snap shut.

Go again. The pink flesh of its neck rubbed raw by the rope . . .

A man comes past. You can tell from his forearms that he's Italian: the neatness of his cuffs, the gold watch, the dark hairs on his pretzel-coloured skin.

'*Buona sera*,' Tina calls after him and smiles. The man turns back, beaming at her.

'*Buona sera, Biondina. Ti piace il Capitano?*'

Tina stares at him.

'Raff,' says the man, his hands forming paws. 'Raff, raff.'

Tina tugs at the neck of her T-shirt, gesturing towards the dog with her head.

'He's sore,' she says. 'His neck.'

'Ah. *Inglese*,' the man says. 'Eenglish — dogs. Dogs—Eenglish.' He pats his heart and laughs.

The man unlocks a metal gate that leads into the yard. The dog howls fiercely. Tina hangs back, afraid, but the man's pretty hand closes over hers and he yanks her in.

'Capteen,' he says. 'Capteen.'

The dog bounds towards Tina, but is brought short by its leash and skids in the dust. The man looms behind her, urging her forward, so close she can feel the bristly swish of his trousers against her calves. In the distance her father calls her name. His voice grows louder. She feels the man's shadow move away and the back of her neck exposed to the sun grows hot. Either side of the chicken wire, her father and the man are announcing themselves in Italian.

'Tina,' her father calls and she runs to him, putting her fingers through the mesh to touch his shirt.

'Daddy!' Her own voice sounds far away. She doesn't recognise it.

'Say hello to Signor Fagandini. You can do it in Italian.'

'I did it already,' Tina says, but she does it again. The man reels off a line of Italian and dog sounds. Tina's father laughs.

'Signor Fagandini says you can play with the dog if you like. But beware: he's a guard dog, not a pet. This isn't England.'

Mr Fagandini crouches to her level and speaks in careful English. 'His name is Captain.' He stands up and roughs her hair. 'He is the boss, eh?' He laughs and walks away. She hears the gate click and the men's feet on the hot gravel grow fainter. Just for a moment she is standing on her own with the dog. Then she pelts down the lane after them.

Up at the hostel their parents unpack a picnic while Tina and Cheryl play adverts on the porch.

'You too could have hair as soft and shiny as mine,' says Cheryl, swinging in practised slow motion round a pillar. Tina enters the frame.

'But my hair's so dry and brickle,' she sighs.

'Just use what I use. New Vidal Sastoon!' cries Cheryl and canters off into a slab of sunlight, tossing her mane.

'Vidal Sastoon. Use Vidal Sastoon!' Tina charges after her.

On the lawn their parents are talking in low voices. The sun beats down, but their mother is hunched as if she's cold. Bread, goat's cheese and a floury salami are spread out on their father's blue waterproof. Tina sidles up on imaginary horseback and dismounts noisily, but her parents don't look up.

'Maybe I was mistaken,' her mother says. Her voice wobbles like a dud high note on Tina's recorder.

'Well, if they're not transferable, I'll take the train,' says her father.

'We'd be back before you.'

'Your choice.'

Cheryl appears. 'Please can I have a Fanta. Pleease.'

Her father doesn't reply. He just shuffles round on his haunches till he's sitting with his back to his family. Tina hovers, testing the grass for somewhere clean to sit her new trousers. Her father wolfs his food down, chewing on one side of his mouth. His bad tooth must have flared up again. Her mother doesn't eat. Cheryl and Tina poke around for something recognisable to feed on. Even the crisps are smothered in paprika.

Tina feels like she does before a thunderstorm. As if an iron clamp is being winched around her skull just above the eyebrows. She tilts her face to the sun and lets it get so hot the skin feels tight. Nuala Godfrey in her class went to Spain and her mother let her wear a Mickey Mouse sticker on her neck for the whole fortnight. When they got back she peeled it off at break and there was a Mickey of pale skin standing out against the brown. So far Tina has only ever freckled. There's a bottle of water on the lawn beside her. She splashes it into her hands and rubs the water on her face to attract a tan. Her cheeks are beginning to burn and she tips the bottle up to her face, misjudges the angle and the last of the water soaks into the lawn.

Her mother hands her a slice of bread and marmalade, but when she bites into it, it tastes all wrong and she spits it out, half chewed, onto the grass.

'I don't like it.'

'Eat up and shut up,' her father says.

'The marmalade tastes funny.'

'It's apricot jam.'

'I hate it. My mouth's gone all dry.'

'Have a drink then,' her mother says.

'I spilt it.'

Her mother sighs. She gives Tina another beaker. Tina tastes it, then gags. Cheryl perks up and mock-retches all over the lawn.

'I wanted water. I feel sick,' Tina whines.

'It's pear juice, Tina, for heaven's sake.'

'It's furry.'

'Beugh!' caws Cheryl, rolling her eyes merrily. 'Puke, puke.'

Her father springs round. 'See this?' He bares the palm of his hand. Cheryl squeals, he slaps and an imprint of his fingers reddens on her thigh. Cheryl's still for a moment then begins to bawl.

'Chrissake,' says her father.

Their mother reaches for Cheryl, but she recoils and starts off into the bushes howling. Tina follows, but Cheryl wedges herself under a bush and screams wordless, beast-like noises until Tina gets bored and returns to the lawn. Her mother is standing up, shaking crumbs from her father's waterproof. Her face is white, like she's in pain.

'Help me clear up, Tinnie, there's a good girl,' she

says. Tina's father is sitting perfectly still. Tina screws the lid back on the apricot jam, turning her nose away and holding her breath to blot out the smell. Her mother packs the food into a carrier bag. She picks the spat-out bread and jam from the grass and bundles it into a paper wrapper.

'Mrs Fagandini says we can store things in her fridge, Arthur,' she says.

'Fine,' he says.

Tina's mother crouches beside her and puts her hand on Tina's scalp.

'You're very hot. You need some shade. Come with me.'

'Daddy, are you coming?'

'Come, Tina.' Her mother takes her hand. The corners of her mouth are pointing down. Tina prods them with her forefinger.

'Smile,' she says.

Her mother shakes her head. 'Tina, Daddy and I have had a bit of a row.'

'About Cheryl?'

'No.'

Tina tests the ground with the ball of her foot. It's good for a cartwheel. Springy and firm.

'Are you going to get a divorce?' she asks and spins off into the cartwheel. Upright again and flushed, she gauges her parents' reaction. They can laugh or they can be cross. It wasn't a real question.

Nobody answers her.

'I don't know,' her mother says, finally.

In the background Cheryl isn't screaming. Her father isn't shouting. There is no noise. Tina tries to fake a casual getaway, but her movements come out all staccato, like their cat, Cora, when she's out stalking, pretending to be a bird. She walks away from her parents as stably as she can, but her legs feel all brittle and stubby. She will walk away in a straight line and she won't stop till she's hit by a car or drowned in the sea.

She crosses the lawn, past the cypresses to where the grass thins out to hard brown ground. To her right are straggly shrubs, to her left a roll of barbed wire and a cement mixer standing empty. In front of her is the high wired fence of the enclosed yard. The dog is in there. Tina doesn't care. She unlatches the metal gate and walks.

Captain rears up and bares his teeth. He's right in her line of vision. She has to walk. She swings her arms and digs her heels in like a soldier, staring ahead at the fence beyond. There is no dog, no obstacle. She will walk and walk and walk. The barks buzz in the distance with her mother's flat reply. She walks on and trips right over Captain's scrawny bulk. Her hand goes out to break the fall and lands in Captain's thin hair. Heat and a pulse she had not expected return her touch. She stays where she has fallen, concentrating on the comfortingly familiar sensation of grazed knees and the new, odd one of petting a dog. She pats and strokes his bony back. Captain mewls and paws at her. His gungey tongue laps at her cheek. He smells dank, doggy, unloved. The tongue rasps and tickles. Tina giggles and wriggles and gets to her feet. His neck is rubbed raw from the rope. She pats.

'Sit.' She presses the base of his spine. He yelps.

'Sit, Captain.'

The dog wrestles into a reluctant crouch.

'Good dog.'

He circles his tether and thumps his tail. Tina pushes him towards the post to get some slack on the rope. Then she unties him and smoothes the hair down round his neck to disguise the sore.

'They never feed you, do they? They never let you play?'

She steers the dog to a trough in the corner of the yard and pushes his head into the water. He laps a little then stares at her. Tina scouts the yard, looking for a stick to throw.

When Kyle Hardie's parents got divorced, Kyle had climbed over the railway railings and waited until he saw a train coming and then lain down on the track. A passer-by had spotted him in the nick of time, jumped over the barriers and swiped him up as the train brakes screeched yards from his head. Lots of grown-ups had come to have sherry at Tina's house and said it was the luck of the devil it had been a local chuffer and not the express, but there was no doubt about it, the child had wanted to die. At seven years old. They shook their heads and said, 'Yes,' gravely when Tina's dad came round with the bottle. Then Kyle's little sister Rosie was paralysed for nearly two years from the fright. She could only drink Coke and say 'Worm'. Tina throws stick after stick for Captain and when they're both tired she sits with her arm draped over his shoulders till the sky turns a runny grey and she feels stiff.

When she gets back from playing with Captain, Cheryl and her parents are sitting in the dusk on the steps of the youth hostel porch. They are sharing a plate of spaghetti and on the tray beside them is one large apple. Why hadn't they called down the garden for her to come and eat? Why was there only one dinner? Where was hers and Cheryl's?

'I'm hungry.'

Her mother must know that. What would there be to make up for lunch?

'Have some of this.' Her mother twizzles strands of spaghetti round her fork.

'I want *my* dinner.'

'This is all there is.'

'But when can I have *my* dinner?'

'You can have this. There's nothing else.'

'Why?'

Tina's father is trembling. His hands are white. He stands up abruptly and walks to the end of the colonnade. He jumps off the edge and heads for the Cyprus trees across the lawn. Tina watches until he is absorbed into their blue shadows and his outline cannot be distinguished from theirs.

Cheryl has taken the apple and is rolling it down the porch steps. Her mother puts a vague restraining hand on her shoulder, but says nothing when Cheryl ignores it, bouncing the apple down the steps and footing it along the path in the direction of Captain's yard. Tina is alone with her mother in the dark.

'If you do it, I'll go with Daddy.'

Her mother says nothing. Tina takes hold of a strand of her mother's hair and winds it like a bandage round her own wrist.

'If I do go, can I still see you?'

'Yes, of course.'

Why does her mother not cry? Why doesn't she say, 'Daddy and I aren't getting divorced. That's for people like the Hardies and the Corretts and the Pughs. Daddy likes to live with us. Snuggle up here and let's get you a plate of your own.' But her mother says nothing, only sits.

'I'll go and tell Daddy then.'

Tina gets up. Her mother stays on the step. Tina walks down the colonnade. She walks towards the blue trees.

'Daddy?'

The trees have sucked up all the light. She moves among them blindly. 'Daddy?'

There's a yelp to her left. It sounds like Captain did when she touched his sore neck.

'Captain?'

Now, hands out in front, she feels her way, like murder, branch by branch. She puts out a hand and a tree flinches. It's her daddy, his fists in his eyes like a baby, shaking. She wraps her arms around his leg and squeezes. She'll tell him now. Tell him that she'll go with him, that he'll be all right. But her chest devil is scratching and pinching her. She has to let it out. She tightens the squeeze on his leg. That'll hurt him. And he won't know she means it. He'll think it's a cuddle, She squeezes. Now she'll tell him what she came to tell him. Now.

'I won't go with you, you know.' Suddenly her fists are out and on his thigh. 'Nor will Cheryl. We won't. I won't go.'

Her father stands where she leaves him, his woolly head rubbing the darkness.

Tina stumbles out to the lighted porch where she finds her mother, still sitting in her summer dress. The skin of her arms is cold. 'I told him I'll go with him not you.'

'I see.'

She climbs into her mother's lap. She doesn't care if Cheryl sees. She tugs at her mother's hair to bring her face closer to her own. She curls a strand of hair tight around her finger and sucks on it. It tastes bitter, but she keeps it there.

The Paperback Macbeth

RECALL A ROOM. This is what Joseph instructs himself to do each time he wakes. Not just the anchors of furniture, but the specific dust and clutter of a given day. It's a trick he heard of years back, in a meeting, or a party pamphlet, on how to keep your mind. How not to rock yourself and sing your way to endless blankness.

He's already revisited both rooms of his grandmother's house where he grew up, her chicken coop where he collected eggs, has passed hours recovering the details of classrooms and lecture halls around the campus where he obtained his teaching certificate, and has returned to his schoolroom, his beloved, vibrant place of work.

Each day so far he's been able to suppress the urge to break his self-imposed rules and revisit his outdoor ceremony of flowers and fires, of drums and fried chicken, that announced his marriage to Njeli. But he may allow himself to, because of last night. He was woken again by the banging of metal doors; that dragging sound, those stifled cries. They are working their way down the line of cells each night, getting closer. Last night the sound was too near; next door perhaps, next-door-but-one, no further. His neck is rigid now, its muscles are lines of fire flaring into his skull. Today he will treat himself and use his imagination to take him home.

A door opens in from the yard. To his left is a pale,

paint-flaked wall. A portrait of our Lord, blue, pink and gold, in a narrow gilt frame, hangs centrally, fixed by a nail. Definitely a nail, not a hook, he banged it in himself. Njeli was outside at the time, pounding maize for their *usima*-meal, her hoarse, low voice repeating the alto part to a local hymn: *nasadiki nasadiki, ninasadiki.* We believe, we believe, we believe in Him.

Don't go to her, he wills himself. *Stay in the room.* Below the portrait stands a cupboard, grey-painted and spindly-legged. Its door sticks. Njeli always swears as she yanks at it and he always scolds her. Inside: two tumblers and a serving bowl. The top of the cupboard is where he sets his briefcase each day on his return from school. He does this now. Puts it down, opens it and removes a sheaf of papers from the Homeland Educators' Development Action Agency, stacking them on top of the cupboard as a reproach to himself should he think of sloping off for a beer tonight before he's read and replied to them. Ah yes. Also inside the cupboard, at the back and wrapped in old newspaper, is a small bottle of grain liquor. His throat scalds at the memory when he finds it. He closes his brief-case and puts his paired shoes close to the open door, out of kindness to Njeli.

The cupboard has a drawer. It holds a paperback copy of Shakespeare's *Macbeth*, given to him by a British actress from the troupe that visited their village and performed in his own school hall before the borders were closed to foreigners. She presented him with it when he went back-stage after the show to apologise for his fellow villagers. They'd cat-called Macduff in the final battle and pelted him with *usima*, refusing to leave the hall with Macbeth slain. He was supposed to be the hero. What sort of play was this that leaves its finest warrior dead? When the actor playing Macbeth stood up warily for the curtain call, they leapt like a football crowd and whistled and cheered.

'Macbeth is the name on the poster,' he apologised backstage, 'so he has to win.'

The actress who played Lady Macduff — so sweetly — turned from unwinding her blue headdress and laughed.

'I am Teacher Joseph Makabe,' he told her. 'It was a very fine performance. Very fine.'

She held out to her hand to him. 'Thank you. Perhaps you should offer them all a class on the text.'

He bared his palms. 'I am the teacher, and even I have no text.'

'Oh!' Her tiny in-breath. That was a detail he'd not forgotten. She'd turned from him and when she turned back, the book was in her hand. 'You must have this.'

Her own copy, with the lines for Third Witch and Lady Macduff faintly underscored in pencil.

'Please,' she said. 'I'd throw it out anyway. There's only four more shows. We're flying back next week.

'I'm obliged.'

And then she shook free her long red hair, combing it with her fingers, saying, 'Macbeth has the finest poetry ever written, don't you think? *She should have died hereafter* . . . So beautiful, not even Lear touches it.'

He wanted to pull up a chair right then and talk more, their thighs not quite touching, but she was called away then by the stage manager in his British army shorts, keen to get the set dismantled. From the doorway, Joseph watched her, high astride the scaffold battlements, unscrewing pipes and handing them down to King Duncan and Donalbain, and then, when the castle was down, wrapping swords in velvet cloaks, stowing them in a trunk soon bound for England.

Take me with you.

How quickly his mind has veered off course. This is why it is vital to do the room-recalling exercise daily. It helps you monitor your levels of concentration. And delay mental deterioration. It's not easy today. Last night's noise has furred him, like a hangover. He returns to the room. The corner beside the cupboard is bare. He runs his eyes over it, finds it thick with ashes, but this is wrong. Why would it be neglected? Njeli is a meticulous housewife. He wipes it clean, begins again at the corner; a stretch of plain wall and a well-swept dirt floor, brightened by a plastic weave mat. Against the wall a little further on is their bed that doubles as a settee by day, spread with a knitted blanket and folded *kikoi* cloths.

Njeli is sitting on it, hands on her knees, her marvellous knees as broad and firm as melons. She clicks her tongue when she sees him, about to begin that conversation again: She didn't marry a man of education to live in a shack. Where is their television? Where is their good settee? Why does she still cook over a fire on open ground like her mother and grandmother? Joseph has tried telling her that any spare money from what he earns should go towards little Joseph's education, and although he's no more than a melon pip yet, inside Njeli, she says, 'What? So he too can fool some poor girl with pretty words and tie her to life in a shack?'

'Njeli,' he says, 'the wealth of life is in here. I insist you listen.' He has the copy of *Macbeth* in his hand and opens it at an earmarked page. '*Art thou afeard /To be the same in thine own act and valour/As thou art in desire?*'

She interrupts, 'Oh, Mister Shakespeare, you are so good for my beauty sleep. Nothing make my eye close faster.' She leans forward to reach for something under the bed, so close to him now he can smell the oil in her hair.

It's a magazine, no, a catalogue for one of the big stores where the *mizungus* buy stuff. She opens it and smoothes the page.

'Mmmm–hmmm,' she says melodiously, like she does when they're dancing. 'This is so nice.' She has her hand on a picture of a settee. She isn't looking at him. 'This looks so very comfortable for relaxing.'

Outside his cell there is a clink of metal. Sweat spreads cold across his back and Njeli is gone. The hatch at the base of his door springs open and a tin food tray is shoved inside. He tries to stay where he is, on the settee with Njeli, but the bones from the guards' food last night are already in his mouth, and his house has gone now too.

After his scant meal, another room comes to him. General Fulam's library. A high ceiling set with two teak wood fans; a walnut table, which gleams so immaculately that the school exercise books spread open on it look improper. The walls of books made Joseph clammy with envy when he was first interviewed for work here, but he knows now that if you try to pull *Paradise Lost* from the shelf, ten inter-linked book spines, hollow inside, will accompany it. Joseph sits on the plumpest sofa. General Fulam's children stand on the carpet before him.

'Let me hear you again,' Joseph says and they respond in soft singsong:

'*Tomorrow and tomorrow and tomorrow*
Creeps in this petty pace from day to day . . .'

To his passing shame, Joseph has timed this recital with the return home of the General, whose boots are clipping down the hall as the children begin. Joseph hears the boots pause at the open doorway. He doesn't turn round but concentrates on nodding and mouthing encouragement at his charges.

'Can you tell me the metre of this verse?' he asks when they reach a breathless, '. . . *sound and fury/signifying nothing.*'

'Iambic pentameters and, um, feminine endings,' Khosi, the daughter, parrots. He knows she has no conception of what this means. He has tried to explain how the five iambs echo the natural rhythm of thought in the English language, how the extra syllable fractures this in moments of intense distress.

'Correct,' he smiles at her, satisfied these alien literary terms will impress their father, who doesn't pay good money each week to have his children exclusively tutored in subjects he himself already knows. Today Joseph is going to suggest, when he sips a mean measure of Scotch malt with the General, that the children enter for the School Certificate in Advanced English. It is a most prestigious examination, but it would require extra tutorial hours. He is still three hundred and eighty *dirhami* short of Njeli's settee. To soften the General, Joseph has planned a surprise. The boy, Bosi, has learned by heart Macbeth's final valiant speech and Joseph has added some warrior moves to accompany it.

The General enters the room, pinching his nostrils.

'Are they progressing well, Teacher Makabe?' Joseph leaps to his feet.

'Oh, General Fulam, you are home.'

The General grunts assent. He stands more than a head taller than Joseph, so that Joseph's eyes are always level with the red and gold decorations of office across his chest. His pale green uniform is never darkened with sweat. In his presence, Joseph feels crumpled.

'Bosi has a new piece,' he offers.

'Proceed.'

The boy takes his position on the carpet and Khosi retreats to her father's side. He puts his arm around her.

'*I will not yield / To kiss the ground before young Malcolm's feet*,' Bosi begins. His legs are too splayed, his gestures stiff and wide. Joseph winces. The General's face is set. He listens to the end. There is a pause. The General steps forward, his hand raised to the boy and Joseph feels himself lift on to the balls of his feet, about to shoot forward and intercept the blow but the General's hand lands on the boy's head and roughs his hair.

'Excellent, excellent,' the General is saying.

Three nights a week now Joseph rides the *isuzu* into town after school to tutor Bosi and Khosi for their Advanced Certificate. The General agreed the extra lessons and they are going well. The settee is already a few weeks nearer, and little Joseph is the size of a tomato now, inside Njeli. This evening the General invited him to stay for a drink, so it is gone seven by the time Joseph leaves. He has missed the minibus that stops at the foot of Daniel Bundu Avenue, where the General lives, and it will be quicker to walk into town and catch an *isuzu* to the village from there than to wait for the next. Perhaps he will go to the market and pick up a chicken for Njeli. Joseph cuts down the broad grass bank that raises Bundu Avenue from Central Boulevard below. At his back are the broad white homes of military officials with their sprinklered lawns and streetlamps. Below him, the scuffed pavements of the town, the dull glass roof of the market and beyond it, the square. He half notices the yellow and red banners hanging there, the mill of people, the bulk of grey army lorries in among the traffic, but his mind is still on the General. It is baffling. When he enters a room, Joseph panics and yet the man is always civil to Joseph, more civil than he anticipates. Today they took their whiskies into the garden and sat a while.

'To learn by rote this way has many benefits,' Joseph tried telling him. He is anxious to stress the wider application of studying English Literature. 'It improves the mental faculties, increases the powers of concentration, can even . . .' he sipped, decided to chance it, 'prevent the deterioration of the brain in later life.'

The General stared at him. 'Teacher Makabe,' he said. 'Poetry is a pleasure. No more, no less.'

'Yes, sir.'

'It is a pleasure no life should be without.'

'Of course. Indeed.'

He has the chicken now, ready plucked, dearer than the feathered birds, but it's a convenience Njeli will appreciate. It is wrapped in paper and warm under his arm. The sun is still hot on his face and he craves a Coke or a beer. The reds and yellows of the protest banners flash in his peripheral vision, but he is keeping his eyes on the bus stand ahead, not turning towards the square. Then his name is called aloud, clearly, three times. He picks up his pace, feigns concentration.

'Joseph!' Suleiman is in front of him, grinning. A laundry bag bulging with propaganda leaflets is strapped across his chest. He holds a placard of Daniel Bundu's head. A black X has been painted through it, obliterating the President's eyes, nose and jowls. The word FREEDOM is printed beneath, each letter as tall as a hand.

'Brother!' Suleiman embraces him. The corner of his placard nests lightly on Joseph's shoulder. 'I knew I would see you here.'

'Brother.' Joseph replies.

'Take this petition round,' Suleiman says. 'We're

missing people coming out of the shoe factories. Here — '
He delves in his laundry bag among the bundles of pamphlets.

'I'm late already. Njeli worries.'

Suleiman stands back from him. 'I haven't seen you at
meetings for a while.'

Joseph shrugs.

'But you are here now.' Suleiman presses his hand. His
palm is warm and dry, but behind the smeared lenses his
eyes are unblinking.

'Suli . . . I teach long hours.'

Suleiman looks past him at the crest of Bundu Avenue's
hill, where General Fulam's house stands. 'So I hear.'

'I have obligations.'

'Indeed you do, brother. Think of Atish. Think of
Horace and Nkomi. Once I knew a Brother whose
schoolhouse was shut down, so he continued his lessons
under a tree. Take the petition.' He fishes in the bag, pulls
from it a clipboard of curling papers and holds it out.

Joseph stands there. Suli should not have referred to
Joseph's school.

'Sign it at least, Brother Speaker.'

Another savage reference. From a long time ago. The
silly passions of college boys. Life is not as cut and dried as
Suleiman would have it. But Joseph takes the clipboard,
signs, returns it, and faces his friend. Suli looks at it.

'Your signature is not as clear as it once was.'

A sudden, united roar erupts throughout the crowd,
and before Joseph has time to reply, his head is bagged,
the chicken knocked from under his arm, his feet are off
the ground. He hears Suli's muffled cry: 'My name is
Solomon Suleiman. I live at 22, Park Buildings. My name
is Solomon Suleiman. I live — '

You call out your name. They used to practise it in

meetings. Your name and where you live so passers-by
will remember. So some good stranger will go to your
home and tell your family why you haven't returned.
Joseph opens his mouth and it fills with the dry dust of
the hessian over his face. His body is hurtling through the
air. When it lands, one twisted foot hits the metal floor of
what must be an army truck, but the rest of him is cush-
ioned by bodies.

Njeli is smiling. She stands in a circle of purple flowers,
groundnuts and eucalyptus leaves. Torch flames flicker
around her. Suleiman and Njeli's brothers lead the dancing
in a wide ring that turns this way and that around her.
Smells of spiced chicken and grilled maize are in the air,
and Njeli's uncle Adi, the one with the gold teeth, who
no one had seen for six years, has arrived from the coast
with an enormous fish that spits on the grill. Njeli's dress
is a miracle; a white satin robe with a turban that appeases
her desire for a Christian wedding and Joseph's own bid
for tradition. It is late in the evening and her skin is pearly
with heat. She begins to shake, arms stretched across the
circle towards him, inviting him in, her body rocking
with longing to be made one with him. Now it's time
for him to kick aside the eucalyptus leaves and crush the
nutshells underfoot, to break the circle and free her into
his arms. He is prolonging this moment. He is no longer
Joseph Makabe, primly Westernised teacher of English
Language. He is a bridegroom. And the wall of noise, of
hooting and chanting that wraps him, comes from the
throats of people who know and love him. Her eyes are
on him. Her mouth is split into the broadest smile he'll
ever see. He steps forward.

The door clangs. This time the dragging sound is made

by his own tied feet being pulled across the earth corridor outside his cell. The mutant squeaks are from his own lips. Where the blindfold gapes across the bridge of his nose he makes out faint green light from an army lamp. Bolts are drawn and his toes now clog with gravel from the yard. The air on his face is so sweet and fresh he is glad of it. Even in this moment. His heart and lungs push at the cage of his chest and his blood is swifter in his veins. So, these are the final sensations of being alive.

They tie him to a post. The meaty sweat of the soldiers who bore him retreats. The air is still. He feels the heat of urine down his thighs. He waits.

The quiet is broken by a measured click of boots across the courtyard. Then a voice: 'Name?' and a soldier's reply: 'Joseph Makabe.'

'Teacher Makabe, heh?'

'Sir.'

'Hm.' The speaker pauses. There is the sound of a metal catch opening, a rustle, then a clipping noise. A flare. Joseph flinches. What are they planning? The rich scent of cigar smoke fills the air. His body loosens. A hand brushes Joseph's lips; the cigar is being put to his mouth. His throat is so dry, but he sucks in, obedient. The smoke is delicious, fragrant and savoury. His mouth had forgotten such possibilities. Then the smoker leans in, so close Joseph can smell his cologne. Quietly he says, 'They gained distinctions in the Advanced Certificate of English. Both of them. I thought you would wish to know.'

Suleiman would spit now, or curse or burst into revolutionary song, but Joseph's last words are, 'That is gratifying, General Fulam. Thank you.'

The boots retreat and the thud of soldiers' feet follows. A conversation is taking place on the far side of the courtyard. Here he is, tied to a post, the last waters of his body ejecting from every pore and the gunfire doesn't come. The sad, hot stench of his own fear rises to his nostrils, jolting him.

'Please?' This is his own voice, foreign to him now. His tongue is thick, unused to speech, but what has he to lose? 'Please, General Fulam, sir?' He pitches the words across the courtyard. 'What is happening?'

The soldiers thud towards him. He's being untied.

'Kiss God's arse,' one of the soldiers says. 'It's not your time. You're being moved on tonight.'

He's crouching on a cold hillside. Soldiers threw him in the back of the van and drove for hours. He was turfed out here, his hands untied and a water bottle placed in them. A rifle was pressed to his spine as a soldier said, 'Don't move till you can't hear the truck. If you do: *Kuh!*' He released the safety on the rifle. 'When you know you're alone, uncover your eyes. After that, it's up to you.' The rifle jabbed him. He heard them climbing back in, the truck doors slam, the engine start. One of them called out to him over the revving, 'If you get to the sea, village called Kawesi, someone there knows you, I'm told.' Dust spurted over him as the vehicle pulled away.

The sun is coming up and turning greys to gold and green. The tiny spiders crawling over his feet, biting his flesh, have scarlet bodies and orange legs. In the distance, light prickles over a wide stripe of water. Such colours. He sees now that the rooms he'd recalled in his unlit cell had muted in his memory. The intensity and range of hues out here on the hill is astounding.

Someone knows him. Someone knows him. He stumbles downhill. His body is weightless. It's as if the mountain shunts him downwards, his legs play no part. As the sun grows, small blue and yellow lamps of flowers shine up at him and he follows their lead until the mountain hits a track and a row of shacks comes into view at the edge of that band of light, painful to the eye, that must be the sea.

An old man squatting by the side of the track at the edge of the village stands with agility as Joseph approaches. He stares calmly at Joseph, then turns his neck and calls: 'Adi? Adi!' He continues, but his dialect is so strong and Joseph so unused to words, he cannot decipher them. A figure appears at a doorway and comes forward to greet him.

Njeli's uncle. Adi. The one who brought the fish to the wedding. The only time Joseph ever met him. And yet this is the man who knows him, tipped off by Lord knows who, Adi won't say, just lifts his head in a tired grin, displaying the gold of his mouth, and leads Joseph down to the sand to rest. Adi sets a bowl of tomatoes before him, so ripe they burst out of their skins and fall apart in Joseph's hands. He is grilling a side of tuna over a fire on the beach. The light is too enormous now. Joseph sits with his back to the sea, head down, pushing the tomatoes into his mouth.

'No,' Adi insists suddenly, as if he and Joseph had been locked in debate, 'you mustn't go back. You must now take a boat.'

He prods at his catch with a stick, poking away at the fish, the fire. And he explains. There is no village to go back to. There is no Njeli. No little Joseph. It happened months ago, soon after Joseph was captured. Adi's voice has tired of emotion. His tale comes out flat, like something that happened to strangers. Soldiers came back, they destroyed the crops, slaughtered the livestock — didn't even take it for food — and torched the houses. What was left of the schoolroom, too.

He wraps some fish in a leaf and puts it on Joseph's lap.

The charred flesh stings Joseph's thigh. His mind will not grasp this news that flows through him like water.

'No. No. This is not possible,' he informs the uncle, but his body flushes hot and cold and he can't move his hand to the fish. Njeli. His schoolroom, too.

'Eat,' Adi says. 'Still, we must eat, where there is food.'

Joseph sits.

Uncle Adi turns back to his fire and spears a piece for himself. Unless Joseph plans to give himself up again to Bundu's army and starve and rot in a pit, he is saying, then he must listen. He must leave the country tonight. Adi has found him a place on a boat. It is a well-run route. And costs twenty-five thousand *dirhami*. Joseph doesn't respond. Adi sucks his teeth in shock at the cost, on Joseph's behalf. Twenty-five thousand, a shocking sum, which Adi will pay on Joseph's behalf for now, in honour of his niece, to ensure Joseph's safe crossing and good quality identity papers. Joseph can send the money when he gets to England. He must return the sum in full within three months. This is not greed on Adi's part, Joseph must understand. The men who arrange the loan will want it back. Not patient men. But Joseph must not concern himself about that. In England they pay a man five pounds each hour to sweep the streets. And a teacher! A teacher qualified, as Joseph is, working in the capital city London can earn eighteen thousand pounds a year. His good friend Kalindi's nephew did that. He works at the Homerton New Technology College in inner London as a mathematics master. It would be better, of course, if Joseph had a friend he was visiting in England, someone who would stand for him as guarantor, because he will be arriving without funds. Without a sponsor they may send him straight back. Does he know anyone?

'Of course not.'

'No one from your teacher-training days? No pen pals from the Water Aid Project in your village? Man, you are a fool. Your English schoolbook sender, who is he?'

'They are from a company. A charity.'

'An educated man and you never bothered to make friends with all these Europeans? You never got an address?' Adi clicks his tongue.

The actress who played Lady Macduff appears to Joseph, turning to face him, one hand untangling her blue turban from her long hair, the other outstretched, holding the book. On the flyleaf is an address in England, but the lettering is faint and hieroglyphic. It slides out of focus. Now she sits on her stool on the makeshift stage in the village hall, leaning forward to stroke her children's hair, in the scene where she teases her children that their father's a traitor, as the Murderers appear in the doorway behind her. The over-ripe tomatoes he's been eating shoot from his gut onto the sand. He crouches, spitting, coughing. Uncle Adi puts his hand on Joseph's shoulder.

'Joseph, no one?' Uncle Adi says.

Joseph lies down in the sand, his arm over his face to protect his eyes. Njeli is sitting on the bed-settee, smiling up at him. She carries little Joseph high in her belly — a sign of good health and vigour. The money for her real sofa is in the drawer of the grey cupboard, tucked inside the paperback *Macbeth*.

Leaf

ONCE, AT A PARTY, when he threw back his head, instead of laughter, sycamore pods flew out. Their helicopter blades whisked the air, and the guests, his friends, lifted their faces and arms to receive them, like stadium stars to ticker tape, then turned and met his eye with smiles as if to say it was only laughter all along. That was the first time.

Then at a family gathering, instead of words, laurel leaves shot from his mouth, dealt like cards from the hands of a skilled croupier across the scattered remnants of the meal, black emerald coats secreting their rich poison.

Next, by moonlight, under dark rain, when a man whispered, 'Would you?' before he could reply he was on all fours coughing up branches of holly. So many branches that they blew along the street, lacerating the ankles of the other man who walked off, as his palms drew the cold up from the pavements into his thirsty veins.

He has come to rely now heavily on the horse chestnut leaf that will slip from his throat, thoughtfully coiled like a slim cigar to avoid pain at its expulsion, and unpeel its broad palm flat across his lips.

Odissi Dancing

HESTER, HETTIE, CALLED herself the Hettalump, unlovely dance administrator, pale lumpish girl with a pale lump of hair braided down her back. She'd been set among the students of the Asian Dance Institute, amongst all this golden skin and hair like pleats of dark silk, to tick registers and collect class fees in a red tin box.

The Space Dance Consortium, which housed the Institute, was hostile ground. The Asian Dance office itself was OK: painted emerald and bulging with boxes of programmes and flyers, but beyond its door lay the realm of serious dance. Behind its Victorian façade, the Consortium spread deep into the bowels of Euston. Long corridors ran down to the offices of authentic dance administrators; genuine failed dancers who pulsed their knees together to work their inner thighs as they typed. The building tripped Hettie up, with its half-flights of steps and blind corners that led to studios and practise rooms and sullen security men who glanced up reflexively at the sound of feet and scowled when it was Hettie, not some gamine in tights.

At night, when the hire rates dropped, the studios were given over to the Asian dance classes. Hettie stayed late in the office, practising the long, unfamiliar names so she wouldn't stumble over them at roll call: Kamaljit Raghuram, Shobhana Banerjee, Ravinder Gopalakrishnan. . .

Ravinder was so beautiful that when Hettie came into Kathak class, tin box and register in hand, she could never breathe. She always slipped in, accidentally-on-purpose, minutes before the break, when the Kathak students were practising the dervish. One by one, the dancers would bow out and spin to the sides of the studio, where they propped themselves against radiators and windowsills until the dizziness subsided. Unni drummed on and the gazelle girls — Daljit and Kamaljit — spun, their yellow silk kurtas twisting round their bodies, thin as whips, until Kamal let herself stumble and fall away, eyeing Daljit to follow her, so the floor was left to Ravinder.

Ravinder whirled so long and fast he blurred, filling the air around him with the blades of his outstretched arms. His hair fanned around his head, his feet beat down and the floor boomed back as if it were a drum skin. When he stopped, the rush of blood and the rich, thick odour of Pratapji's classroom made Hettie's head swim; incense, sweat, and the sweet aniseed herbs on Pratapji's breath as he greeted her briskly, irritated by this nightly intrusion of administration on his teaching.

The woman in the sari shop in Tooting was gentle to Hettie as though she had special needs. She plucked a size thirty-eight blouse from the wire basket and said Hettie was not a forty-two at all, it was the fashion to wear these blouses tight. Hettie paid her three pounds. The blouse had been stitched by hand, and instead of buttons at the front, it closed with a row of hooks and eyes.

'You may take classes too, if you wish,' Pratapji had said when Hettie started. 'Staff don't pay. Sit in on some sessions. See what you fancy.'

Hettie watched the Kathak first: the melting bodies, the slim headed girls with their gold fingernails. Impossible

even to think of attempting it. She gave Kathakali a go
for a couple of weeks, standing behind four lean hippies
in loincloths who worked earnestly and dripped sweat
copiously onto the floor.

'Come to my class,' said Priyaji, Pratapji's wife, small
and round and fragrant as an apple, just like Pratapji.
'Odissi is the dancing of the temples, it is the most beautiful and classical of all the Indian dances. You will like it
very much.'

It was the clearest of the dances. Hettie found she could
stand at the back and pick up the steps. Priyaji went over
and over them. The jutted hips, breasts and neck of the
tribung, the square-bodied *choh.* Each move was rehearsed
fifty times for Kamaljit and Daljit to perfect the exact
angles of their torsos, their eyes, the curve of their arms
and necks. Repeated so often, it was possible even for
Hettie to get the gist. She stared, never at the mirror, but
at the back of the sturdy, reliable girl in front of her, Jhoti;
saw only the rope of her red-black hair, the dark, plump
arms, forgot herself. But now Priyaji had announced that
students with 100% attendance were classified as a troupe
and expected to perform for the Diwali Festival at the
Commonwealth Institute. The thought of hettalump-
ing her way through a display of grace made Hettie's gut
burn. Priyaji refused to understand her excuses.

'Do you attend my Odissi class?'

'Yes.'

'Then you are an Odissi dancer. You will honour me
and perform.'

In her alarm, Hettie mistraced her way through the
tangle of corridors back to the office, and blundered into
the basement Ladies'. This was the domain of the ballerinas, who pinched their hipbones and poked at their hair
in the mirror. They had scent-marked the toilet stalls with

their raw notes of deodorant and vomit, and covered the cubicle walls with their body commandments: *students who put on more than three pounds during the year should be asked to leave; fat is a weakness of mind and has no place in dance*, and in capitals in thick black ink: *BURN THE FAT*.

Hettie looked at the spread of her own white flesh across the toilet seat. It appeared to have no connection with her. Washing her hands, she watched the ballerinas bashing in and out of the cubicles, lighting covert fags, cocking their legs up on the basins to get a full stretch. Where on those stringy limbs were the cells that enraged them? When Hettie moved to the hand-drier, her body lumbered along too. She blanked it. It was a balloon and she was a grain of rice rattling around inside it.

The sari she bought in a shop behind the street market in Balham. This time the shopkeeper was not polite. He pulled on his moustache and shifted his comfortable body away from her. When she pointed out a sari in the glass case, he shook his head, punched out a number on his mobile and conducted a pleasurable argument in Hindi or Punjabi, she didn't know which. Hettie waited and when he finally rang off, he looked annoyed that she was still there.

'Lady, you cannot buy this. It is only for weddings,' he said, covering up the silver and red sari with a plain green cotton one. He took a leisurely look at her. 'I think you are not getting married.'

'The thing is, I need one in red and silver,' said Hettie, 'for Odissi dancing.'

'Yes, I know Odissi dancing,' said the man. He rolled his index finger round the heavy gold chain at his neck. 'You dance?'

'Sort of.'

He opened a drawer, pulled out a sari length of synthetic white lining cloth, bordered in red. 'This is the Odissi sari.'

'I wanted, I thought something more, with some embroidery.'

'This is the Odissi sari.'

The man took a pole and went outside, unhooking bright satin dress suits from a display above his shop door.

Hettie stood at the counter. A smell of fried lentils and garlic had worked its way into the shop from the room behind. Outside, a van backed up, blocking the doorway, and when it drove away, the fruit stall opposite had been stripped to a blue metal frame. The stallholder dismantled it swiftly, clanging the pieces on the ground, calling to his mates. The sari man came in and out, squeezing the dresses in their cellophane onto a rack. Hettie went up to him. 'I'll take it,' she said.

'Twelve pounds.'

He folded it small and put it in a brown paper fruit bag.

The dim, wood foyer of the Commonwealth Institute was empty. It smelled of rubber and detergent, like schools. Hettie felt as though she had eaten an enormous meal. Like nights in adolescence, when she'd run back for orchestra practise or choir through the dark park, weighed down by solid food that her mother set before her like a challenge. Plough through this and then get a life. She carried her sari and blouse in a plastic bag. Five to seven already. She'd got off the bus at the wrong stop in the dark and had run the length of the Cromwell Road. They'd all gone in. There were so many fire doors and staircases, and no signs. Then, turning a corner, she heard faint chorus noises coming down the stairs, chatter and laughter, and

Bhangra music played on a tinny tape machine. The landing above was pooled with fluorescent light.

The girls of the Odissi class were up there. They'd wedged open the double doors with fire extinguishers and opened the windows to create a breeze. Jhoti and Shobi were leaning out of the window, having a smoke. Other girls were bent over handbag mirrors laid out on the desks, applying kohl to their eyes, and scarlet lipstick, under the poor strip lights. Some sat on tables having their toenails painted by friends. The proper dancers, the soon to be professionals, Daljit and Kamaljit, had pushed back the desks and were practising their steps, intoning the rhythm, '*Drin tiri kiri taka, Nak tiri kiri taka, Ata ata ata dini.*'

Hettie found a quiet corner and changed swiftly. Her skin was sticky from running. She should have bought the forty-two. The blouse cut into her arms, squashed her chest. She rubbed foundation over her face, applied mascara and lipstick, and then leaned against her desk, a little out of breath and at a loss.

It was nearly time. Priyaji arrived in a heavy wool coat, smelling of winter, looking at her girls, asking to see a good *choh*, a good *tribung*, adjusting an elbow, a neck, with her tiny index finger. Then she was gone and Kamaljit stood in front of Hettie, aghast. 'Get ready,' she said. 'We have to go down.'

'I am ready.'

Kamal's forehead creased into a pretty frown.

'Have you no jewels?'

'Uh, no.'

The Hettalump bulked up inside her as the Odissi dancers closed in. They had hold of her arms and legs. Their hands were in her hair and on her face. Jewelled fingers plucked at her dull lining cloth, 'Come and look at this!' One was scrawling graffiti across her arm. The chemical ink rose to her nostrils. Her feet were being trussed, her neck choked. She sat rigid for the barrage of taunts, but they didn't come. One by one, the dancers and their actions cleared and took form. It was Shobi who had her hand. She was copying the henna patterns of her own feet onto Hettie's arm with a sepia marker pen. Kamaljit had clipped a heavy web of silver round her neck and was pushing bangles onto her free hand until Hettie was armoured to the elbow with dozens of bracelets, slender as threads. Jhoti was buckling leather collars hung with brass bells around her feet.

No one had ever dressed her — not since her mother squeezed the shrunken necks of jumpers over Hettie's too-large head and pulled her hair up into a ponytail. She had assumed that a woman's touch always makes your eyes water with pain, but felt now only the tickle of Shobi's pen and cool hands in her hair, deft with years of decorating the bodies of friends.

'You bring flowers?' Jhoti asked.

'No.' She'd brought nothing. Nothing for anyone.

'I'll find some.'

Daljit, of the sleepy film star lids, clinked over to Hettie in all her jewels. Her delicately ringed throat, the dark skin around her cuticles as she dipped her kohl brush, filled Hettie's vision. How could anyone look immaculate close-up? Daljit the Beautiful, painting dough. When she smiled her teeth were wet, her head smelled of the savoury oil combed through her hair.

'Don't blink,' she said. The kohl felt cold.

'You should get one, Daji,' Shobi was saying. She looked at Hettie. 'Where d'you get it? It's the proper Odissi sari. Priyaji has one. Daji's gold is all wrong.'

'So?' said Daljit.

'Done.' Shobi capped her pen and pulled her cigarettes

from the waist folds of her sari. Flowers bloomed on Hettie's hands, there were rings on her unringed fingers, eyes in her palms.

'It's beautiful.'

'It's good, innit? I do everyone. I've got a steady hand. Think we've got time for a fag?'

A woman with a clipboard came to the door looking pasty and frazzled, as Hettie must look when she barged in on classes, the grey, business-end of dancing. They were to follow her down. It was time. The dancers lined up. They tinkled and chimed. Thick hanks of crimson chrysanthemums hung down their backs. Someone patted Hettie's neck, said, 'There you go,' and the girls behind her slipped off the desk to join the others.

Walking was strange: loaded with bells, weighed down with bracelets, neck taut with all the metal around it and the hairdressing above it, Hettie could feel her every bone, every joint, as if they were newly implanted. Her body seemed springy against the heaviness of her costume. She tried a *tribung*. It sank into place against the weights. She lifted a jangling arm to her hair, touched something soft. A scattering of brilliant yellow chrysanthemum petals fell across her shoulders.

They edged forward into the corridor, blinking against the gloom. The walls were lined with posters advertising Kathak and Odissi troupes. The dancers stirred ahead of them, chirruping against the clipboard woman's gestures for silence. The shuffling bare feet paused as each dancer bowed to a poster of a vast and stately woman in voluminous green silk. Broader than Hettie's, her bare calves grew into the pleats of her sari, solid as trees.

'Pushkala Chandiwala,' sighed Jhoti. 'The best Odissi dancer in the world. I'm going three times next week.

You want to come?' She put her long gold fingernails up and touched Pushkala's feet for luck.

'Yes,' said Hettie. She brushed Pushkala's sturdy midriff with her fingertips.

They were ferried into the dark well of the wings, ripe with glue size and incense and then before Hettie had time to feel sick, to seize up, they were on the stage. Against the haze of light, Hettie saw Jhoti's back in front of her as it always was in class, and Priyaji's reedy voice started up from the loudspeakers: *Namahami, brik sha raja tum*. Hettie slapped her foot against the floor. The floor rang back, resonant, like the skin of a drum.

Ultimate Satisfaction
Everyday

G REG MASON WAS a loser. He flogged dry dog
food door to door round the outskirts of Romford
and would have cocked-up even this career had he not
married the boss's daughter, Eileen, because one unusual
night he felt able to ask for her hand. Her father, glad to
be shot of the sniping little mare, rewarded Greg with a
sales franchise in Emerson Park; an easy, salubrious territory that earned him the resentment of fellow salesmen.
But after her father retired, Eileen barged in on the business with a thirst for wealth that Greg found unseemly.
She booked herself onto deal-closing seminars and then
exploited her new found knowledge, hogging the phone
when orders came in, pushing protein-enriched treats
that Greg was sure played havoc with dogs' kidneys. She
upped the price each time new stock arrived. When business dwindled she blamed him. One sub-zero night she
locked him out of the house in a game that turn humour-
less. To drum initiative into him, she said. But he gave
up and went off to kip on a banquette in The Mariners,
handing two months' Peak Fitness Doberman rations to
the barman by way of thanks. For Eileen, that was the
end.

Greg's solicitor lost him custody of the kids. He saw
them twice a month, in charred play parks and cinemas.

They spotted food on his tie and traded Yu-Gi-Oh cards with each other under burger-bar tables, ignoring his questions. When they parted, his eldest said, 'Laters,' and wouldn't return his hug.

One afternoon he was delivering to a leafy detached on Woodlands Avenue when Eileen's car pulled up at the mansion next door and Greg's kids tumbled out. That unscheduled glimpse of their uncombed heads and restless limbs kicked his heart. He was gearing up to greet them when through the hedge he spied a man younger than himself belting a ball in the air, and saw the blue curve of a swimming pool. Still, they were his kids, so he called to them. Their footsteps stopped and he heard his youngest whisper, 'Dog alert. Hurry. Or he'll want to talk to us.' The gate clanged as they headed for the pool.

Greg drove away, not back to his rented room above a shop on the Hornchurch Road, but down to the Thames at Rainham, his childhood stomping ground. He parked where the road ran out at the entrance to the municipal tip. They'd grassed over the mountains of landfill since he'd last visited. A smell of toasting rice from the Tilda processing plant dominated the air. On either side of the water, factory chimneys steamed and machinery whirred, softer than the birdsong from the Purfleet sanctuary a mile away, as if industry itself ticked by unmanned. No need of human interference. No need for men like him.

Downriver, some wag had placed a skeleton frame of a diver out in the water, as if caught to his waist in the mud. No doubt the council had commissioned it. They had ever-wilier ruses for squandering Greg's tax. Some self-appointed Thames Gateway Artist-in-River-Residence probably landed himself a fat grant for cobbling together found objects from the council tip or shoreline rubbish and called it sculpture. But though he wanted to berate it, he found himself drawn to the diver, and stood a while, watching the tidal water run through the mesh of his torso, swilling about in the empty cage where his heart and guts should be. The late afternoon light on the wide river, the sounds of the birds and machines and the tide all filled his head and distilled his thoughts to this:

He sought one thing. One thing he was proud to have done in his life.

He'd lived all his life in Havering, this sleepy rural second cousin of a London borough, and that placidity seemed bred inside his bones. At Hi-Pro motivational conferences he'd met salesmen who'd moved out from Bow and the Isle of Dogs. Living here was a sign of making good. There was an edge to them, a pride born of having escaped the city. And there were the ones who'd moved in from outlying Essex villages, hungry for all those Romford doorsteps, every one a sale in the making. But Greg was not edgy, not hungry. Until now, Havering had suited him. He'd been quiet and kind and satisfied all through his life, but that was from disposition, not choice. Should he have fought for Eileen? Would a bitter custody battle have shown his boys a depth or quality of love they doubted now? He tried to remember how he'd filled his time before she'd commandeered it. Hours at the run-down gym in the outhouse of The Admiralty, weight-lifting. He'd been strong back then, in body. Perhaps that's what Eileen had liked. Perhaps she'd imagined that strength ran through him. Why, he'd been so physically powerful as a single man that once he'd lifted a car to free a child trapped beneath.

Greg breathed in, stepped forward towards the river. At his feet, a thousand washed-up water bottles and coffee cups looked up at him like a stadium crowd. A sudden calm infused him. That was the One Thing. He had forgotten it until now, but he had saved a life.

~

Back then his energy outstripped his patience for exercise. He'd done two circuits that night, all his usual weights upped by ten, and not felt tired. The other gym-jocks invited him for a pint and he turned them down, not wanting to blunt the fizzing health he felt. It was November, early dark. He crossed the yard onto the steep main road. Outside Costcutter's a car pulled up and Kerry, Dean Fletcher's girlfriend, got out. Her knew her by sight. Prettiness masked by acne, wet-look curls, long legs.

He watched casually, his eye drawn simply because hers was the only movement on the street. The spill of light from Costcutter's window framed her, adding potency to her ordinary actions, as if she were in a film. Kerry went to the boot of the car to fetch something. As she did, the rear door opened, her little girl scrambled out and toddled in front of the car. Greg was about to call out for Kerry to watch for her when he realised the car was rolling downhill. It nudged the child and she fell in its path. The car's front wheel rolled onto her hair and her trailing fur hood, trapping her, inching towards her soft wide face. All this in seconds as he sprinted towards them. Kerry screamed into the night: 'Oh, someone! — Oh God!'

Greg reached them, squatted, lifted the car clear, not aware of its weight, just the hot strength flooding through him. Kerry pulled her free, face buried against the child, saying, 'Ashley, bubba, wake up, talk to Mumma.'

He released the car and it seemed light, bouncing as it landed. When he stood, it felt like he kept on rising and rising until the world were navel height to him and he could run his hands over its surface to make it right. Now other people, scenting crisis, joined them: the checkout man from Costcutter, waving a lollipop at Ashley, an old woman quoting out-of-hours doctors' numbers by heart. The cashier pushed the lollipop against Ashley's lips. Her eyes opened, blank, staring past her mother to the sky, then she opened her mouth and shuddered. Her scalp was bald in patches, and bleeding, but the checkout man said scalps do bleed a lot, his brother's did when he got attacked, and it looks worse than it is, see her neck's moving and she's breathing. Kerry kept thanking him for the lollipop. She didn't thank Greg. She moved away from the car into a dim side street, the pensioner at her shoulder, advising.

For a moment the cashier looked like he might ask Greg something, but some teenagers started shouting in his shop and he went after them. Greg stood alone in the street with Dean's car. The power that had brooded inside him was gone. He felt clean and his skin stung, like after a day in the sea and sun. That night he asked Eileen to marry him. Weeks later, her dad set him up with the new franchise and they moved to Upminster. He hadn't seen Kerry or the child since.

How had he not carried that with him over the years? He wasn't sure he'd even told his children. He and his wife weren't given to reminiscing and the boys were not the curious kind. He must have told Eileen the night he proposed. As he stood looking out across the wide river, he thought perhaps he had and that she'd slid her cool hands over his biceps, bringing his mind back to her, where she believed it should be.

He turned to head back. Along the Thames, beside the Tilda loading jetty, the fleet of dumped concrete barges had shifted over the years. They stood half-submerged now in the river sand, hulls pointing at the sky. In childhood he had imagined the barges solid and wondered how a boat made of concrete could float. Now that they were disintegrating, he saw it: their skins were paper thin, their frames no sturdier than the diver's mesh. His father used to walk him here some Sundays, pointing out the council plaque that said the barges had formed part of the Mulberry Harbour, played their part in winning the war. He'd heard that disputed in recent years, as though the barges had fancied themselves in their youth and now their crumbling frames shed doubt on previous honours.

Seventeen years ago he'd lifted her free. He got into his car and headed back along the service road from the tip towards Rainham. Ahead of him, the A13 ran on stilts over the salt marshes, feeding traffic into London and out to the ferry ports. He scanned the cars for green 'L' plates. Ashley could be gunning along nicely on that road overhead right now, her head full of a trip to Paris or a West End show.

The image pleased him. Over the following days he developed it, gave her a new dress on the back seat of the car, various occasions for wearing it. Not for Ashley a life standing on the footbridge, fending off the slipstream of the Eurostar as it hurtled through Rainham station. She'd be inside the train, a glossy mag open between her pretty hands. She'd escaped death. She'd not be one to let life grow over her like weeds.

His own boys remained morose, uncouth, as Ashley, the daughter he'd never had but now laid claim to, blossomed. He was there at her graduation when she tossed her mortar-board into the air where it freeze-framed. She smiled delighted when he, not a patient, walked into her surgery. But why stop there? 'Hey Greg,' she breathed into the mike from the stage at O2. 'This song's for you.'

The Fletchers lived three floors up on a council run in Harold Hill. It had taken Greg eight days to find them. He'd contacted many Fletchers in the old neighbourhood, a sack of Hi-Pro Dog at the ready, as an excuse. At this door he got a feeling, a settling round his shoulders. This was where a sympathetic Kerry, an ever-grateful Dean would introduce him like a lost relative: This is Greg. He saved your life when you were small. He'd like to meet you now if that's OK.

A middle-aged woman opened the door. It took him a moment to realise she was Kerry. Her drenched curls had been replaced by a helmet of purple hair, and the acne had given way to smoker's lines.

'Kerry. It's Greg Mason, remember me?'

'Might.'

'I wanted to see Ashley.'

'Ash,' Kerry called through the flat, 'Got call.' No welcome, no sign of surprise, but she stood aside and let him pass into her orange lounge which housed a cabinet, a sofa spewing foam and a tin dog-bowl.

Kerry turned on him, fingers flicking unseen fluff from her sleeves. 'You sort her meds before you're out that door, all right? She's back forty-eight hours and already she's doing my nut. And I want her housed cos she ain't staying here. Got that? This is *my* home and she's—'

A girl came into the lounge. She had her mother's dark curls. On each cheek was a weeping sore, like a second set of eyes, larger and brighter than the small dull ones above them. She went to the sofa and lay on it, pulling her jeans down low on her hips to reveal a hard ball of a belly, which she kneaded, groaning and twisting.

Greg stood feeling cumbersome, searching for the right comment. He landed on a genial and soothing, 'The midwife's on her way, is she?'

'Can you stand in the doorway, where you ain't in the way,' Kerry said. 'She ain't in labour, she's coming off methadone. Ain't you even read her file?'

'Sorry,' said Greg. She must think he was a medical man or from social services. Her misunderstanding pleased him, showed she saw in him a man who helped others, changed lives. He wanted to be that man and turned to watch Ashley with what he hoped passed for tender, professional assessment.

Ashley yanked at her jeans, trying to undo the waistband, then gave up and her hands went limp. 'It's freezing in here,' she said.

'It's up full whack, Ash,' Kerry replied.

'Oh, I'm not gonna make it!'

Ashley rushed from the room, bent double.

Kerry studied him. 'You're new, ain't you? What was you before?'

'Sales,' he said. 'Pet foods.'

'Hah!' Kerry squealed.

She retrieved a key from her sweater, unlocked the cabinet and took out a bottle of liqueur. It had a stick of sugar running through it, shaped like coral. When she'd poured two shots she locked the cabinet and tucked the key back into her bra. 'Not a good game this, is it? Need a bit of this and that to see us through. Suck it down.' She handed one to him—a challenge. He knocked it back. Like candied fire. It was years since he'd drunk anything but beer.

From the bathroom, Ashley retched and moaned and flushed.

'Ain't you got questions?' Kerry asked.

'Would she like to be readmitted?'

'What? To Holloway?' Kerry screeched a laugh, caught his confused eye, screeched again. 'Dunno, pet shop boy, shall we ask her?'

'I meant hospital. What's she on?'

'Nothing. Lost your notes? They cancelled the meth script soon as she got out. Don't give her nothing to tide her over cos she'd only flog it. She got to go up the GP, but she won't.'

Ashley came back into the room. Her jeans zip was undone to ease her bloated belly. She looked up at him with both sets of eyes, then her head drooped and she shivered.

'Hey,' said Greg. He took off his jacket to give to her.

'Oi, she's burning up. You got to keep cool, Ash. You only think you're freezing. Open the window, Key-worker.'

Greg opened the door to the balcony, onto bland, summer air. The estate spread out beneath him, its chalk and smoke buildings, the broccoli trees of Duck Wood to the East, and traffic snaking south towards Romford centre with its glass land of shops and bars. It wasn't that bad a place. It didn't deserve such helpless attitudes from him or Ash or Kerry. In the late afternoon light it looked full of possibilities.

'Hey Ashley, come and stand out here,' he said.

'I got the heebies.'

'Well . . . have them out here in the sun.'

'Bloody hell.'

But she stumbled out towards him, still grinding her fists into the swollen rock of her belly. He gripped her arm. Her body was surprisingly compliant; it fell against his. He righted her, trying to steer her round so he could stare into her eyes, but she wouldn't meet his gaze. She kept squirming and keening about her bellyache, like a spoilt child. The diplomas and silk dresses and concerts, even her ruddy driving license detached themselves from her and sailed from the balcony, sailed down like the clothes of a spurned husband. All his plans for her, all she might have been, dispatched towards the blue van up on bricks in the yard below, from which music with a brain-stopping beat thumped back at him.

'Look around you!' he said. 'I gave this to you.'

'Eh? What?'

'Look!' He shook her gently, he thought, paternally, but she wailed. The pillowslips drying on the balcony opposite, the music from the knock-off motor below, even these should seem marvellous to her.

'Get off me. I'm dizzy.'

'Oi!' Kerry came to the balcony doorway. Greg let Ashley go and she crawled inside to the settee. Kerry beckoned Greg in, but blocked his way so he had to squeeze past her.

'Reckons Social recruited him off a bloody pet shop, Ash,' she said. 'Mind your step or he'll kennel you.' Up close she smelled of sweat and bleach. The skin under her eyes and at her chin hung in frail loops. Greg had to fight the impulse to tuck a finger up under the flaps, as he did with dogs whose faces hung that way.

'You ain't her Keyworker. What are you?'

'Greg Mason,' he said. 'Dean's mate from school, remember? The car outside Costcutter's. Ashley fell under the wheel. I lifted the car.'

'What?'

'I lifted the car so you could pull her free.'

Kerry's eyes flickered. 'I ain't saying you're lying,' she said, 'but I don't recall. She was a terror. We was in and out Queens' A&E so much they almost give us her own bed. Ash, remember that time you was running on top that Spitfire at Hornchurch aerodrome and you fell and that squaddie what caught you split his arm up, breaking your fall?'

'Nuh,' said Ashley.

'You was only small.'

Now she'd begun, Kerry went on describing all the others like him, leaping to preserve Ashley's treasurable life. Pig-thick of him to imagine his action had made him unique.

As Ashley rocked, a bull terrier appeared from behind the sofa and trotted to the empty bowl. It yapped at Kerry.

'Tough,' she told it. 'Ain't got none. You'll have to wait.'

Greg walked past them into the hall. The sack of dog biscuits he'd brought as an excuse to call was still by the front door. He carried it through. Kerry was on the sofa now, embracing Ashley, and the terrier was up on the cushions with them, snouting at Ashley's hair.

Greg opened the bag and shook some biscuits free. The dog jumped on them, the choppy exertions of his tail a frantic mimic of Ashley's rocking.

'What you'll find,' said Greg, 'is that this is comprehensive life assurance for your pet in pellet form. Health. Vitality. Balance. Ultimate satisfaction everyday.'

The words came easily. He explained how the simple daily discipline of selecting this food form over the bewildering array of inferior choices available in today's supermarkets would enable them as owners to get the most from their dog and would benefit their pet throughout his days.

His spiel had never run so smoothly. When he'd finished Greg set the sack beside the door, and though they had their backs to him, he bowed. He'd found her. He'd provided this small service. He could leave now and he'd be OK.

Things like Meat

W ENDY NORMAN WAS perfect. She had a kilt. She had Persil-white knee socks that her mother never turned inside out so she could get a couple of extra days wear from them. Her house had a storm porch. Her brother was Steven with a *v*.

The first time Wendy came to stay at Kit's they sat in their nighties watching TV. Kit crouched on the sofa, willing her parents to say something parental like, 'Come on girls, it's time for bed,' but they didn't. Kit's mother lay stretched in front of the fire like a cat and her father drank tea from his pint mug, swallowing clearly. At the Normans' house, Wendy's bedtime was seven-thirty and Steven's was eight o'clock. It went up by half an hour on their birthdays. Kit's own daughter, Wendy, or maybe Gillian, she hadn't decided yet, was going to have a bedtime plan stuck to the fridge with a magnet and filled in each year with a different coloured felt tip pen. Her pocket money would go up each year on budget day, like Wendy and Steven's did. Kit wouldn't eke things out till Christmas and birthdays either, she'd be like Mrs Norman and say, 'I'm just popping into Marks and Sparks to get some socks.'

It was way gone nine. They should be in bed. Instead they were watching a film called *Psycho*. It was OK at first, with a car and some man with his mother, but now there was a woman in the shower with no clothes on. Please, Kit prayed, *please* say something like, 'I don't really think this is suitable for you girls,' but her father was about to say something unbearable, something not for young ears, she knew he was, he was leaning forward in his chair and the tendons in his neck were twitching like they always did when he was on the brink of outwitting the telly. Kit bartered wildly in her mind: OK just say, 'Disgusting!' like you're really disgusted.

'Tits.'

She didn't even hear the sentence that surrounded it. The burn stretched from her ears to her throat. She couldn't look at Wendy. It was something about not seeing enough of the tits. 'Do you want to go to bed?' she whispered.

Wendy nodded. Her eyes were wide with terror at the woman's naked outline against the cloudy curtain. The woman was lifting her throat to the head of hot water as they crept upstairs. That night Wendy Norman cried herself to sleep and Kit lay awake in the divan next to her knowing it was because her dad had said 'tits' and because they'd stayed up too late.

It was three months before Kit's dad went away for a week to a conference in London and she could finally dare to have Wendy over to sleep again. After school, they played out. Kit liked playing air raids with the boys in the back lane, but Wendy wanted to bat a tennis ball against the wall. Kit watched. It was reassuringly dull, and she liked the way Wendy's kilt bobbed when she jumped for the ball. Kit's mother even called to them from the kitchen door, just like Mrs Norman, and when they got in she brought tea on trays so they could eat it on their laps in front of *Look North*.

The man on the news was live from a train station in London. Announcements squalled over his report. *These books look innocent enough . . .* he said. The books were scarlet with no writing on the covers and long white tabs dangling from them. They looked peculiar. The newsman had stacked them on a pedestal on the station platform so he could touch them without bending over. *If you saw them on a busy platform such as this, you'd probably pass them by. But look closely!* He flipped open a cover: *This could easily be hollowed out and filled with explosives. To set it off, simply pull this tag . . .* The screen snowed. *We've used confetti to demonstrate . . .* In the hands of people like the IRA, the newsman told them, the confetti could blow your arm away or wipe your face clean off your head. The death toll was rising. He stared out of the screen at them. *Is London at war?* he asked.

When Kit's uncle Gordon was posted to Northern Ireland, everyone talked about the IRA. Auntie Laine was so relieved when he was posted back. Kit imagined her clapping as she unwrapped him. Her mother said she could never be married to a man as long as Gordon, his legs got in the way. He was ten inches taller than Kit's dad, and if he was around when they went to stay with Auntie Laine, he took Kit to play on the long noses of the practice tanks outside the barracks.

Everything was perfect. The bread was sliced—luckily her mother hadn't had time to make her own—and had Shippam's paste inside. Wendy Norman had eaten her rock cake first and grouped the burnt currants neatly on the lip of her plate. As a safety measure, Kit told her, 'We have to go to bed after this, my mum said. She's very busy so she might not come in and tell us, but we've got to.'

It was *Doctor Who* next. The Doctor and an old man friend of his gave the Daleks the slip down a flight of steps by a window full of shop dummies. The Doctor cried out and flung his friend to the ground. The dummies' wrists fell open, spraying bullets at the spot where the doctor had stood, shattering the glass. Daleks trundled to the top of the steps.

Upstairs, with the lamp off but the daylight pouring in, Kit ventured, 'I'm glad my dad's not here.'

'I'm glad too,' said Wendy.

Kit's stomach churned. She lay still.

'I love it when my dad goes away. We get to stay up late,' said Wendy. There was just a trace of accusation in her voice.

Mr Norman had sideburns and hairy hands and wore a wedding ring. Kit couldn't think of a reason he might have for going away. He ran a tool hire shop on Aitken Road. When Kit's dad sighed because the grass was too high, Kit urged him to hire one of Mr Norman's sit'n'mows. 'It's an idea, I suppose,' was all Kit's dad would say.

'Don't you hate it when they fight?' said Wendy.

'What?'

'When they fight and it's always your mum that cries, isn't it?'

'Yes,' said Kit.

There was only the one time, and her mother hadn't cried, but had led Kit downstairs and said not to worry, it was only a bit of a squabble about Auntie Lainey. Kit's dad was still on the bed with no pyjamas, his legs tucked up to his chest and his thumbs in his eyes like an upturned beetle, curling and turning and grizzling away.

'Why don't *they* ever cry?' said Wendy, tucking the quilt up under her armpits. 'It's always your mum.'

'Yeah.'

'Sunday, my dad got my mum against the wall cos the meat wasn't cooked properly,' said Wendy, 'and he still had the electric carver in his hand. Steve had to pull him off. It wasn't even her fault, she'd never even cooked a joint that size before.'

In Kit's mind, Mrs Norman's back was arched over the radiator, her hairdo squashed against the wipe-clean walls. Mr Norman's hairy hand looked enormous. Kit looked over at Wendy. Her nightie was so white it made the sheets look yellow. Wendy stared solemnly back at her and stroked the bobble on the end of her plait.

'And he says, 'Stop crying woman'. Does yours say that?'

'Yes.'

'Does your dad do it cos of things like meat?'

'Yes.'

'And he says she looks a right prozzie in the morning in those shades.'

Mrs Norman dropped Wendy off at school every day in her car. She wore a pink sheer headscarf and coral lipstick and sometimes huge brown shades. She always said, 'Cheerio,' and looked like she was going off somewhere fun because their house never needed tidying.

'We don't have a car,' said Kit, and Wendy let it pass as a reply. Kit tried to steer the conversation onto common ground.

'Don't you hate it when your mum wears silly hats?' She had a wealth to say on this subject.

'I'm getting sleepy. I can't talk because my ears pop when I'm tired,' said Wendy, 'Night night.'

Kit dreamed she was walking home from school with Elsie up the road and Douglas, the boy with the hearing aid who was adopted until he got given back. Elsie and Douglas were ahead of her in the back lane. Panic flooded her body. She knew when they went round the corner they'd die. She tried to call out to them but her mouth was empty. The backs of her legs were wet. She didn't want to turn the corner when she got to the end of the lane, but little Douglas and Elsie were disappearing round it ahead of her and she had to follow him. When she reached the corner, they'd disappeared. A red sports car with its hood down was parked on the pitted tarmac. A man was slumped over the wheel, his head pushed through the windscreen, blood trickling down the shattered glass onto the bonnet. It was her job to lift him free. She knew it was her dad. Then into the road marched a dummy, taller than Gordon, in army trousers with a rifle. Its eyes were glass blue and, though she tried not to, she looked into them. The dummy sprayed bullets at her through his eyes and mouth.

She awoke soaked through. Perhaps her hot water bottle had leaked, that had happened once, but she found it with her toes, still bulging and cold. She got up, peeled her wet nightie away from her skin and crept past Wendy Norman to her mother's room.

Her mother put a T-shirt on her and said to hop in beside her, they'd sort it in the morning. Her voice was stretched and slurred with sleep. Kit nestled against her, away from the cold patch of sheet where her father should be.

'Do they have books in London?' she asked.

'Millions of books. The British Library.'

'Are there books where Daddy is?'

'Lots of them. It's a university.'

'But were there books at the train station?'

'At King's Cross?'

'At the station.'

'I doubt it. Not at the station, no.'

'Tell him: don't touch them.'

The warmth of her mother's belly spread down her back. Her mother stroked her hair.

'I will.'

The sun was high and the radio on. There were sounds of brakes, a car horn and an engine ticking over in the street. Kit looked out. Mrs Norman stood with the passenger door open. Wendy was climbing into the back seat. Mrs Norman smacked her on the calf and Wendy turned round and said, 'Thank you for having me.' Kit's mother came to the gatepost. Her hands and front were covered with flour. She stooped to hug Wendy, leaving a white hand mark on the back of her scarlet cardigan. Mrs Norman, in her headscarf and lippy and huge brown shades, slid into the driver's seat and, with a radiant smile to Kit's mum, said, 'Cheerio.'

Moleman

I FIRST HEARD OF the Moleman when I had no plans for my life. When just the thing to fill a day was a walk along the canal to look at his home. Everyone should have a spell of no plans in their life. It leaves you susceptible, wide open.

For once rumour was not exaggerated. The Moleman's house was more shocking, more of a vertiginous dream, than I'd been told. A corner plot of a down-at-heel East London square. Every window was masked with yellow newspaper. He had moled his way down through the garden, past the foundations . . . right under the house. Its fragile balance made me look up. I was afraid it might unhook its moorings and float away.

The Moleman and I evidently saw eye to eye on this, and I was impressed that he had come up with a solution. He'd attached butcher's hooks to the corner of each wall, high up near the eaves. Steel guy ropes, tied to the hooks, were pulled taut into the earth below, creating a makeshift tent of that Victorian pile. My admiration deepened.

His garden startled me. I stood on his patch of pavement, peering down into the steep pitch of mud slopes, shored up in random spots with old fridge doors and sides of cars. It had to be forty-foot deep. No final ground was visible. I felt sucked in. Lured. I had to close my eyes and turn my back on it before I could walk away.

After that I found reasons to walk past although it was a six-mile round trip from my flat. But, as I say, in those days I had no plans.

His butcher's hooks fascinated me. He'd fastened them to the corners where the two walls met, just below the guttering. They were nowhere near a window and there were no skylights in his roof. How had he reached them? He'd dug so deeply beneath the foundations that he couldn't possibly have used a ladder. There was nowhere to foot it.

No one, bar the council, had ever seen him. But everyone knew of him, and the stories they could tell! He'd once been a grand philosopher, a pamphleteer. He'd had thousands upon thousands of his pamphlets printed in the sixties, which proclaimed his vision of utopia, but when nobody bought them he went underground.

I stared more closely at his windows after I'd learned that. The sheets of print were too small to be newspaper and had aged to a pleasant buttery yellow. They were his pamphlets, looking out at the world in place of him. I tried to get close enough to read a line or two, but he'd had much to say and had said it in a tiny, compressed typeface. What a marvellous man, to take his spurned philosophy and insulate his house with it.

He was a compulsive tunneller. He'd tunnelled for miles under the streets of Hackney and De Beauvoir Town. Some blamed him as the reason London Underground make excuses never to extend to Hackney: the district might sink into his labyrinth. But it was not until City bankers began to gentrify the square and discovered the cause of their subsidence that the council intervened. Until then they'd been lackadaisical about his activity.

Prompted by bankers, council officials called round to

complain three times in a row and when he didn't reply, they fretted! Hackney council, who'd rather grind you to corn and scatter you on the ground of some illegal cock-fight than show compassion, were concerned that he was missing, possibly injured or trapped in one of his tunnels. They sent Special Constables in. The constables searched for three weeks by torchlight, confirmed the tunnels ran for seven miles or more, but found no trace of him or any other living thing. It turned out he'd fancied a holiday and gone to Belgium.

I had a portrait in my head of him. A short man, shoulders stooped from all that tunnel dwelling. Pale, with thinning hair. Then one night I was coming home from drinking with people I barely knew, a little wild on wine and walking streets I didn't recognise, when I saw a lighted window, high on the wall of a house. I looked in. As I did, a breeze whisked up, steel guy ropes hummed, and I realised I was outside his home. I stared through that window. The walls behind were mottled yellow—maybe pamphleted—a bare bulb, nothing else. Then he walked into view.

Of course it was him. Of course he was more marvellous than my imagination. His shoulders were not stooped from tunnel dwelling. They were vast from all that digging. His hair was thick, buckling silver that ran down to his chest and his hands, as he lifted them to rinse a bright red plate — he was washing up — were enormous spades. Perhaps he sensed my focus because he suddenly threw open the window and lurched forward, those hulking shoulders filling its frame. I lifted my hand to greet him from the street below, wanting to speak. I had already decided I would accept if he invited me in. He saw me and raised his spade hand in salute. I stepped forward, face lifted to his light. He moved out of view. I waited, expecting his feet on the stairs, watching his door for an hour. When it didn't open, I understood.

I went home and slept. Next morning I woke early, dressed and went outside. I took a shovel to the front garden. The soil was knitted tight with grass and didn't yield with ease. I made an incision in the turf, a metre square, and lifted it clear. I dug. Soon the sun was up, raising wholesome scents from the soil and my scalp. My muscles warmed and loosened to this good, honest toil. I dug until nightfall and then I dug more, down through the layers of silt and stone and clay. And I've dug on, uncovering more earth.

The Tenth Mother

LATE IN JANUARY after a flu that had grounded me for two weeks, I took my first wobbly walk up the market. There was a new stall, so thick with customers chatting and laughing I assumed it was another Burberry seconds' stand — their factory's near where I live — but as I approached a breeze lifted its green and orange leaflets into the air. One blew onto my chest and I peeled it off: *Do you have space in your home and heart for a child like Midge?* Midge's poorly Xeroxed eyes burned out at me from under a brutal haircut. A woman with hairbraids reached across the stall and touched my arm. 'You interested in fostering or adoption?'

'I. I'm on my own.'

'No problem,' she said.

It was a day of swift cloud and sharp sunlight, colder than it looked. Her words misted the air in front of her. She hovered, smiling. 'Some kids, you know, they prefer a house without a man in it. You want to have a think? Give us your address?'

By February I'd forgotten all about it. I left the letter unopened for a week — council crests usually herald tax demands or news of bin-day changes. When I got round to reading it I realised the meeting was that night at Council Hall. As I folded the letter back inside its envelope, I noticed my hands were shaking and my heart was caught high in my chest.

The room was hot. Self-serve orange squash and custard creams were laid out on a table for prospective parents, like a whiff of the children that had eluded us so far. I looked at my competitors: a nervous Asian pair, holding hands; a white couple, not quite concealing a recent tiff, and a man in a skullcap, pacing. A woman scurried in, unpicking the knot on her headscarf, and he pulled her into a seat. As I passed, I heard him instructing her: 'You are not to tell them that.'

The rest were single women, noisy, like the ones at the stall. They all seemed to know each other. When the adoption counsellor walked in, they wiped biscuit crumbs from their lips and smirked like teenagers.

'Fosterers through the door at the far end of the room, please,' she said. 'Adoptions stay here.' The exodus startled me. Only the couples and myself remained. The council woman propped herself against the front of her desk and smiled. 'Welcome,' she said.

Babies, of course, don't exist. There is no such thing as an unwanted baby. We were to banish all thoughts of bringing home a bundle, she said. But there were *children*, she eked the word out, who were ready for a new family, and right now the council were in the unprecedented position of having more children than prospective parents. Hence the campaign.

We were one, the couples and I, worked by the child-placement officer like a lung. We slumped back at the lack of babies, puffed up when she told us how rare and fortunate we were to be needed at all. As we gathered our stacks of handouts and application forms at the end, I asked why fostering was so much more popular, it seemed odd.

'Money in it,' said the officer.

In March I was visited. Just a preliminary. The inter-viewer, Terry, had a big bum in a floral skirt, exhausted hair and plastic specs. She stood in my lounge and sniffed before she sat down. The smell of new polish caught in my throat as I copied her.

'And what do you do for a living, Dawn?'

'I'm an administrator.' Didn't she have my application form?

'For . . .?'

'Hatbox Theatre Company.'

She frowned as if this gave me dubious status. Perhaps she thought theatre lax, that I lunched with pretty actors and lay on sofas choosing plays. All I do is payroll and endless futile bids for revenue funding.

'In the accounts department,' I improvised. She ploughed through my biscuits, and when Eartha came in and rubbed against my leg, she said, 'Be prepared you might have to give up that cat if a child has asthma.'

April. No news.

A memory has circled me all month of running on the cliffs at Sennen Cove when I was nine. I tripped on a stone, was thrown forward and there, inches from my jarred chin, where my feet should have been, was the plunging darkness of a tin-mine shaft. The chance of a child is like that. For years the longing is crusted over, unnoted, but when it appears it is a sudden lightless cleft.

I got my next assessment in May. Dilly and Joe from Hatbox prepared me. Friends of theirs had been through it, been turned down, no reasons given. 'For God's sake, don't tell them the truth,' Dilly advised. 'Tell them what they want to hear.'

What was my ideal child in an ideal world?

One that wanted to live with me, who blossomed in my care. *The right answer, but also the true one. Some say blue eyes, blonde hair.*

What did I do myself as a child when I was unhappy?

Perch on damp rafters under the eaves, ignoring all adults calling my name until they forgot I was lost and returned to their drinks. Sulk a little, I said.

Have you ever been pregnant or had an abortion?

No. *Bravo, said without a pause.*

Why aren't you married? Have you ever had a relationship with a man? Do you prefer women? Do you hate men? How would you feel about adopting a boy? A blind boy? A boy who couldn't feed or clothe himself? A boy who'd never learn to speak or read or write? Look at all these books in your house, she said. Are you truly telling me you wouldn't care?

Late June and Terry's on the phone. 'Congratulations!' she says. 'We've found you a match. Are we hot on the case or what?'

They have a boy. A terrific little chap. Douglas. He's had a few troubles in his time and been badly let down. He wants a mum with no other children around and he doesn't want a dad. He likes reading and football. Douglas will need a secure and loving environment to help him come to terms with past experiences. She sounds like she's reading from a script.

'What experiences?' I ask.

'The male figures in his life have not been positive. Drink problems in the family, one too many step dads. Been in care. He gets on with his mum, but she's ill and she can't cope with him anymore. She's ready to release him for adoption.'

'When can I meet him?'

'Next Thursday at four,' Terry says. 'He'll be back at the Home, after school.' She hesitates. 'Do you still have that cat?'

'Yes. Is that a problem? Is he asthmatic?'

'Not as such,' she says. 'We'll see.'

The first Thursday in July, Derek from the Home and Terry take me to the bottom of the garden, where Douglas is digging sand under the climbing frame. Someone has scalped him for the summer. His hair has barely grown back. He wears pebble glasses and his red shorts are too snug. When Terry calls to him, he ignores her.

'Playing hard to get,' she says.

Derek calls heartily, and I call too. His head turns. I have never seen a look like it. Belligerent longing. He approaches me, squints up.

'Zat my next mum?'

'Yes.'

He does a speedy head swivel to check the others aren't watching, then tucks his hand in mine. It's dry, sticky. It hot wires to my chest.

'All right,' he announces. He cocks his head butchly and leads us into the house.

He is standing in my hall. Terry's just left. She has 'settled him in' by spending half an hour nursing my biscuit tin. Eartha is high on the dresser among my mother's pottery, face flat, tail bristling. 'Remember,' Terry says on her way out, 'RAG's the way: red light, amber, green.'

This is social services' code for coping. Green's things which aren't OK but you let pass anyway — too much telly, broken toys, wet beds. Amber's a warning. You have a word, threaten punishment next time: vandalism, nicking from your purse, staying out all night. Red's no-go: drugs, self harm, soliciting.

'Guess he's a bit young for some of that stuff,' Terry says doubtfully.

As the door closes behind her, Douglas sighs noisily and wriggles his shoulders as if to shake free of her. I can't help grinning. He catches me.

'Douglas,' I say, 'If it feels funny calling me mum straight off—'

'S'all right.'

'Well, if it does, you can call me Dawn for now.

'I've had eight mums an' a birth mother.' He offers this up like a plumber telling me he's found the leak. 'M'I in there?'

I have decorated the door of his room with posters of the Hammers, his team, and a brightly painted wooden name sign. He picks up his kit bag. His legs are stalks, but he walks like a heavy, shoulders bunched, hips stiffly swaggering. I want to wrap him into me.

'Yeah,' I say casually. 'Take your time.'

August. At some point we have to start living the way we intend to go on. It can't be burgers or jammy bread every night. I take Doug with me to the supermarket. My plan is for us to cook together. If he's personally supervised the chopping and steaming of vegetables, maybe he'll eat them. I stand in the veg aisle looking at mange tout and broccoli, at pyramids of carrots and red onions.

'Doug, aren't these colours fantastic?' I say and turn to him. He isn't there. The panic rises through me like a fog.

Between the tinned beans and cereal I find him with a middle-aged woman in elegant clothes. She has his arm pulled up so high he's on tiptoe. I swing my trolley aside to sprint to them, hear it clang into the end display behind me. It takes forever to reach them; she has already hit him across the ear. The woman turns on me. Her face is purple.

'Your child?' she says. She is brimming over. She releases Doug. He stands between us, eyes bright as a drinker's. 'He assaulted me.'

'Did you just hit him?'

'He touched me.' A quiet explosion. Her voice is like gravel. 'And he knew what he was doing. If you can't teach your child what's right or wrong, then someone must.'

'You can't go round hitting children,' I say. I pull him to me. He twines around my leg. She grabs his wrists, yanks him free.

'You don't touch ladies like that,' she rasps. 'If mummy won't stop you, I will, you hear? And you,' she says to me. 'You're the disgrace.'

She picks up her basket of expensive leaves and cheeses and walks away.

I want to pursue the woman, to sit over coffee with her and agree on principles of child-rearing. I feel a crazed homesickness for the good, lone-woman food she had chosen. There are people around us, freeze-framed, tins poised between shelf and basket. They are looking at me. Bad Mother. I want to tell them he's not mine.

Dougie's asleep and I'm on the phone to Dilly with a glass of wine in my hand. First time I've let myself off the reins since he came, although he already knows I smoke. He seems to find that comforting. When two bills came at once after I'd cut my hours at Hatbox, I was sitting staring at them in the kitchen. 'Shall I fetch your fags, Dawn?' he said.

'The things he comes out with,' I tell Dilly. 'His Cardiff mum, she still loves him, sends him cards and stuff, but he's too much of a handful. His posh mum—somewhere in Clapham, I think, I'm not sure—she handed him back when she found out she was pregnant. Can you believe that, Dill? Like he's a faulty car seat. The longest he's been with anyone's eighteen months. We treat animals better.'

We went kite flying today on Parliament Hill. We rode the train from Hackney and I let Douglas guzzle Wotsits on the way. He complied with the kite, for my benefit. When we got it up, I gave him the ropes, standing behind him, like a real mum, helping him steer. The sky was dull before thunder and the kite glowed out against it, orange and green. With my hands over his, guiding, we tugged the strings until it did a little loop the loop. I whooped with joy.

'Dawn,' he said. 'Don't. Enthusiasm's sad.' What a long word. Where did that come from? I love him.

In September I stand here seeing what he's done, and I'm telling you it feels like the bones have shot out of your body. Like your blood's replaced by razors ripping through you, letting the you of you, the familiar, dog-eared, unchangeable heart leak out into a puddle on the floor, and God knows what's left to deal with what's happening right now. I know he needs me. I know I'm his last hope. I know he's testing me and I hope to God that if I pass this test we're through the worst. I know Eartha was only a cat and he's a boy. I don't know the right thing to do, don't know what I want to do—yes I do—I want to beat him. I want to whack him and whack him, but he knows already what terror is and that particular wisdom hasn't helped him much, so I hold out my arms.

He walks into them, arms rigid at his side, pushing his skinny frame against me. It feels like hugging the devil.

His energy saps into me, prickling like an allergy, but I hold him. This is a child, I tell myself. Look how small his arms are; his head.

'D'you want rid of me?' he asks.

'No,' I lie.

'M'I all right then?'

'Doug, you can't do what you did,' I say. I grip his shoulders too hard. He's getting it. 'When people hurt you in the past, you didn't like it, did you?'

'Dun care.'

'You didn't like it,' I tell him. 'Now we're going to make a promise to each other. I won't ever hurt you, or let you down, and you won't hurt animals or children at school. Is that a deal?'

'Dun mind.'

That night he falls asleep against my arm as we're watching TV. I carry him upstairs, limp and weighty against my chest. I lay him on his bed and fold the covers over him. As I'm backing away, his hand flips out of the quilt, catches on my shirt, pulls me down.

'Dawn,' he says. 'Don't send me back, will you? You're-so-nice-I-love-you. I'll call you mum n'all.'

He burrows his stubbly head under my chin. I breathe in the hamster-nest smell of him, stroke the bird bone ribs down his back.

'You can stay forever and ever,' I say. 'And I'll always be here. Stay till you're so big we have to knock down the walls to keep you.'

In October I change my mind.

The Piano Thrower

LINDA SHARMA LOOKED like Snow White would if she'd got stuck in that forest for twenty years, skivvying for dwarves: alabaster skin threaded with veins, jet hair now lustreless and stacked in a keeling beehive. She stood on her side of the porch smoking a Regal from the packet she kept tucked in the sleeve of her twin set.

Tish hung out on the Pottingers' stretch of porch in the hope of catching Linda there. Sometimes Linda offered her a ciggie and then stared, a bit glazed, and said, 'No, I suppose you don't as yet.'

Today Linda was in theatrical mode.

'Never marry an Indian,' she advised. 'You ever saw a drunk Indian throw a piano down the stairs?'

Tish shook her head, wishing she had. Wonderful sounds came through the walls from the Sharmas' bedroom in the house next door to Tish's. Wails that crescendoed into song at times, sobs at others. Last night was screams and thuds and sounds of furniture on the move.

Linda sighed darkly. 'Pride of my life it was, that piano. Lovely piece.'

Tish looked at her shoes. Many things were the pride of Linda's life. Usually her dogs. Or her younger waistline, which Sharma could put his hands round either side when they married, and his fingers met easily in the middle. Once Tish had been named the pride of Linda's life. And once, Linda's parrot. It was never Linda's tiny, violent, Indian, merchant seaman, drunk of a husband, Sharma.

Tish's personal favourite pride-of-life was Linda's previous waistline. They liked to re-enact it together, squeezing their own hands round their waists. They were doing it as Sharma walked up the path. He stopped when he came upon the obstacle of Linda. Tish watched him. He stood straight as a rod, a tremor running through him. His eyes wobbled in their sockets, and there were purple marks under his skin as if someone had patched him from within.

Linda caught his hands as he raised them to shoo her aside. She steered them over the low wall and before Tish knew it his fingers were around her waist and squeezing, conducting their tremor through Tish's own skin. She pulled in her tummy muscles, drew in her breath, but his fingers didn't meet. Sharma laughed abruptly and took his hands away, shaking them as if he had no dryer. Tish felt she'd just failed some test she'd never asked to go in for.

'Do me now, Sharma. Do me,' Linda said. But Sharma just sucked his tongue noisily and went inside the house.

'Did he really throw a piano down the stairs?' whispered Tish.

'You calling me a liar?' Linda pinched the burning stem from her cigarette with her bare fingers and tucked the dog end back inside the box.

Tish wanted to say, 'He's only small,' but wasn't sure Linda would take it, so she improvised. 'He must be very strong.'

'The man's a veritable tiger.'

That night Tish stood in her knickers in front of the wardrobe mirror and put her own hands round her waist, forcing them to meet. They left a ring of crushed red skin when she had to let go. Later, the screams flung themselves through the walls, right into her bed. Tish's dad came and sat by her pillow. The muscles in his legs looked spring-loaded. Linda cried: 'Oh Sharma, Sharma, don't hit me. No, no.' There was a crash and then a silence so still and deep it seemed to Tish that her father moved in slow motion through the dark bedroom.

Tish put her ear to the wall. Sometimes the comforting drone of telly worked its way through, always sounding like a western. There was nothing. She hoped for a sound. She thought perhaps she could hear Linda breathing, but maybe it was just the plaster shifting inside the walls.

'I'm going in,' her father said. 'Stay here.'

But Tish slipped down the stairs behind him and out into the front garden past the low run of fence that separated their semi from the Sharmas'.

Her dad opened the Sharmas' glass door and called aloud.

'Hello. Pottinger here from next door. Everything all right?'

In this house with its velvet paintings of collies on the walls, its air of bacon fat, his voice sounded Southern and pompous. Tish wished she could get him to start again. But the door to the kitchen opened, and Linda's mother, Doreen McCluskey, came out slowly, in her nightie and housecoat already.

There was no sign of piano damage. Mrs McCluskey must have repaired it all. Tish had been in their kitchen once and seen Linda's mother on her knees, papering the bottom of the wall.

'She has to do it every week,' Linda said. 'The dogs scratch and splash from their water bowls.'

'Why don't you put tiles up?' Tish had asked.

'Tiles? She does it every week.'

Now her father was walking towards Linda's mother, his hand extended, radiant with neighbourliness.

'Good evening, Mrs McCluskey!'

He looked too keen, too missionary. You had to downplay enthusiasm with families like Linda's. Even Tish had worked life out that far.

'Is Linda all right?' he asked.

'I s'pect so.'

'May I check?'

'Well, I wouldn't.' Mrs McCluskey glanced at the banisters as if they might back her up.

'But may I?'

'Well she's in her room.'

'We heard shouting.'

'You want a look at Linda? In her room?'

'Yes, if I may.'

Mrs McCluskey consulted the banisters again.

'Top of the stairs,' she said. 'At the front.'

'I know which is her room,' Tish's father said, taking the stairs two at a time.

'I'll bet you do,' said Mrs McCluskey and smiled as if something at last was entertaining her.

On the landing her father told Tish to go home. She compromised as far as the half-landing by the bathroom and watched from the corner, stroking her face against the woodchip walls. Her father moved slowly towards Linda's bedroom. Silent, like he was creeping up on her. He stood with his ear to the door for some time then squatted and put his eye to the keyhole. The way his backside strained against his twills as he strove to balance and see made her stomach squirm. The word for that was squeamish. He was going about it wrong. You don't skulk. You burst in. You lift her square and high onto capable shoulders and bear her away to a wholesome home — for now Tish's own would have to do. There, in time, Linda would learn to trust again. Her hair would regain its sheen and her cheeks their bloom. She would probably start calling Tish the daughter she never had, the pride of her life.

There was a sound of feet in the hall downstairs. Mrs McCluskey passed into the lounge and soon the television was on, laughter rattling like sudden rain beneath them.

Through the walls someone groaned.

'Sharma? Linda? You in there?' her father called softly. Tish crept onto the landing. Something icy nipped up her back even though the fear was straight ahead.

'Linda? You there? You all right?'

Another groan which rose to a wail. 'Oh Sharma, Sharma, don't leave me.'

Sharma's voice, which Tish had only ever heard through the walls at night, answered, gruff and slurred, 'Shut up, bint.'

'Don't leave me.'

Her father turned, shooing Tish back downstairs. 'Let's go. She sounds hale enough.'

They were halfway downstairs when the screams brought her father belting inside the way he should have done from the first. Tish flattened her spine against the woodchip. It poked at her. Through the open door she saw Linda thrown down on the bed, her neck twisted as though she were trying to look backwards through the wall into Tish's house. Her quilt was oyster sateen and she wore a peach negligee. Her hair was down. A fringed bedside lamp ringed her body with amber light. She looked like a movie.

Her father must be well inside the room. She couldn't see him, only the shadow of a man, vast, bearing down on Linda, cutting off the light around her throat. Linda's head moved slowly and she groaned. Her long hair fell across her face.

'Sharma!'

'It's me. Mr Pottinger. From next door.' He didn't sound like a hero. He sounded on the brink of a lecture. Linda propped herself up on one white arm and lifted a bottle to her lips.

'He beat me!'

'Get up.'

Tish edged inside the room. The air was sickly with old Regal smoke and a sour lemon perfume that should have smelled clean but didn't. Opposite Linda's bed a dresser overflowed with perfume bottles and underwear. The mirror was newly broken. A wooden stag from a family of three deer—Tish had the identical set in her own room—was upended in a pot of cold cream. She went to him and pulled him out, wiping the cream from his antlers with balls of yellow and pink cotton wool. The mother and baby deer waited for him on the windowsill beside Linda's bed.

'Get up, woman!'

'Dad,' whispered Tish. Sharma must be somewhere in the room, holding his breath in a cupboard, ready to spring. Fear zigzagged up her back again.

'Dad!'

But her father was standing over Linda. She sat on the bed, still posed like a movie queen and tilted the bottle at him.

'Vermouth,' she said. 'Have some.' She waved the bottle at Tish. 'Ah, pet. Here too. Have some. Vermouth.'

'I can't.' Tish's voice was dry. It barely came out. Her father smiled at Linda and held his hand out for the bottle. She passed it to him. Tish watched as he opened the sash window, and emptied the wine into the garden. She heard it trickling indiscreetly onto Mrs McCluskey's roses. Linda swayed, eyes rolling from Tish to her dad.

'Bugger him.' She tipped back her head and made a hacking noise. From her mouth came Sharma's deep roaring tones: 'Bugger the lot of them. Bugger you all! You silly bint. You stupid, stupid bint. You cack.'

Linda lifted the mother deer from the windowsill and tossed it across the room. It split in two against the broken mirror.

'Oh!' Tish hadn't meant to make a noise, but Linda heard it. She looked at Tish for sometime as if deciding what to do with her. At last she looked away.

'Take,' she said. The rest of the sentence was too much for her. Her arm waved vaguely at the windowsill.

Tish stood there.

'Goan. Take,' Linda insisted.

'She wants you to have her ornament.' Her father's voice was impatient, familiar. It let her move. She crossed the room to him. He took her hand. Her other hand closed over the smallest deer, her fingers rubbed its buds where antlers might grow. Behind her Linda was wailing now, her voice climbing into a song: 'Hallways on my mind. You were hallways on my mind.'

'Look,' her father said. Outside the night was navy blue. The streets were wet with fast, light rain. On the far pavement, a small man walked two dogs, his back rod straight. It was Sharma.

'Good evening,' Tish's father called down to him. Sharma looked up. He showed no surprise that his neighbour was in his bedroom. Without breaking step he gave a neat, naval salute and said, 'Good evening' back in a delicate voice as the dogs led him forward. He passed under the soda glow of a streetlamp, which made his black hair shine like new.

Two Minutes

THERE IS A HAILSTORM outside, gale force. It shakes the windows. The children stand and look out, tummies pressed to the radiator, chanting: 'Hailgale! Hail-gale!'

She stands in the doorway watching them, knowing the exact moment when their joy at the rhyme will turn physical and become a rolling of bodies on the heap of cushions they have dragged onto the floor. It happens just as she predicts, and though she is glad they are rapt in this tumbling and hooting, a chill runs through her that she has such control over them, such knowledge of them, that she could predict to the quarter second when they would peel themselves from the radiator as they did and cavort.

And into this chill comes the return of an abrupt memory that she owes her neighbour Mrs Ellis fifty pounds, so she stops fretting about the children and frets over Mrs Ellis instead as the wind spins round and sends hail flat smack against the windows. Mrs Ellis has been on at her, by email and phone, asking for her fifty pounds back, and truly she hadn't meant not to repay it, but she forgot and forgot so often that the act of returning the money became difficult until she had a sort of block on doing it and even when she remembered she would put it off in favour of another more trivial job which was ridiculous because why punish Mrs Ellis for lending it in the first place when she badly temporarily needed it and perhaps Mrs Ellis is in a similar situation herself and now needs the money back and wouldn't hound her for it if the need weren't urgent? Though she suspects this is not the case as Mrs Ellis has only the one fat son and a husband who runs his own vending machine reconditioning service, unlike her, coping with two alone, two she wouldn't change though they can be a handful, like when they sat in the middle of the kitchen floor in a tall white expensive heap of washing powder, flour and sugar, and innocently turned to her aging face and said in piping voices: 'We concocting.'

But no, the fond recollections of the girls' previous misdemeanours won't dislodge this sudden anxiety she feels at owing Mrs Ellis fifty pounds. And it's funny, isn't it, how you can owe it for weeks, weeks that slip into months, and then suddenly the guilt of owing hits you like a gale force and you know you must act on it – after all, she's had the money to pay back in a drawer for two weeks for heaven's sake, in a brown envelope marked 'Mrs Ellis' because she'd thought to maybe get a Thank You card to accompany it and then couldn't find one she liked. She realises she is putting her boots on in the hallway as she thinks this. She realises she is going out right now in this filthy weather to return the money to Mrs Ellis and this is exciting because it will give her back some energy, some of the energy she had lost since owing it because these things sap you unawares and you find if you can't do one small thing the others won't budge either, like the laundry which is her own tall white misdemeanour heap.

But the girls. They are rolling around in their jumpers and tights, all gleeful, like a glimpse of children before you have children of your own, when the roundness of their bodies and the softness of their hair seems exotically endearing. Now she will have to smash this scene and cram their feet into boots which are still cold and stiff with dampness and probably too small now—that's one of the small jobs that got stuck behind Mrs Ellis's fifty—measuring their feet for new shoes.

And their coats are still wet through, hanging on the radiators. Mrs Ellis is, after all, only ten doors down. And it seems ridiculous. Her own mother did it. What is it with today, that you can't pop up to a neighbour without cramming the kids into uncomfortable, drenched and icy clothing and yanking them out of the house, creating maybe an hour or two now of sulks and plaints and twining voices, just to deliver an envelope, just to tuck it through a letterbox, because she doesn't want to ring the bell or chat on the porch or be invited in for goodness sake!

She opens the door and the hail and wind come in at her like bailiffs. She has to use some force to push it shut again. The girls are now taking turns to bury each other under the cushions. She calls to them, 'Girls,' but her voice is ahead of her. She thinks she is about to say, would it be OK if she just popped out to deliver a letter, but her voice retracts it. She has never left them before. Not for two minutes.

They are older now of course. This is what she keeps forgetting. The tall white heap incident was ages ago. They will be safe. Cushions for heaven's sake. What could go wrong with cushions? And then she thinks what could and discovers herself shouting at them to put the cushions back on the sofa and they crawl out from under them, flushed and surprised and compliant, chorusing, 'Sorry mummy,' in a practiced tone. And she finds herself giving them the choice. She must go up to Mrs Ellis's and she must do it right away in this weather, and would they like to come—it will be exciting with the hail they can catch on their tongues and maybe they can try leaning into the wind, which the younger one considers for a moment, she sees it in her eyes. But the older one curls on the sofa shaking her head vigorously, 'No,' she says, 'No thanks,' as though her mother often popped out and left her the option of staying home alone.

'But I am going,' she says again. She expects some reaction. No, no thanks, the older one says again, and she is shot forward to their teenage years of tossy hair and self-absorption and benign indifference. The younger one cottons on. 'Are you leaving us here, alone?' 'Just while I run to Mrs Ellis's,' she says. 'You can come if you want.'

'I don't want,' the girl says, dive rolling over her sister onto the far side of the sofa. 'It's fine, Mum. It's fine.'

'I'll only be two minutes,' she says.

Then she goes into the kitchen and opens the drawer, which sticks so she has to wedge her fingers inside and root around for the envelope and prise it out. But after that delay she is ready and there is actually nothing stopping her. She opens the door and the bailiff wind is back, spraying hailstones on the hallway floor.

'I won't be long,' she calls but already there are cartoons on. She hears their music and tinny voices, and arching above these the breathy reassurances of her only two children, 'We know, Mum. It's fine.' And she steps out. The door flings itself shut behind her. She looks back through the lighted window but they are too small, too low on the sofa and the window set too high in the wall to get a last glimpse of them, and anyway the hail is heavy now, driving down, and the wind whisks all manner of hard and tiny objects up around her eyes, so she is forced to bend double, her bare hands holding the envelope and the house breaking away from her, with her daughters in it, like an iceberg, breaking away and floating, gathering speed as Mrs Ellis's house in all this weather zooms to a vanishing point miles away on the road ahead. Miles away and years.

Mudlarks

K YLE SAT ON a stack of Thompson's *Local*s in the
passenger seat of his dad's lorry, doing his home-
work on his knee. He'd had all Easter to do it but he'd
not felt right.

He read again: *Define history. (Ask yourself: What is
History? and put your answer in the box below.)*

The lorry shunted forward in the morning traffic. Kyle
waited until it stopped then wrote: *History is when you
Google the olden days to find out how pig-ignorant and disgusting everyone was until nowadays. Like, mega poor children were
Mudlarks when they looked in the river for things to sell, only
mainly there was dead dogs in there and also the Mudlarks stuck
their feet in sewage to keep them warm.*

He looked up. His dad's eyes were screwed half-shut
against the early sun. The muscles in his forearms swelled
as he released the handbrake. Lots of people admired his
dad's forearms. He always told them it took years without
power steering to get that Popeye look. Kyle checked
what he'd written and heard Mrs Kendrick's voice asking,
'Is that all you could think to put?' He added: *Like in Topic
of the Week — Medicine, we learned medieval doctors thought
people got ill because of their Humours and what mostly came
out of their orifices, such as phlegm from Phlegmatic people who
are cold and wet and cowardly. Now we know this isn't true.*

His dad taking him to school today was a first. He'd
have felt brill about riding in the lorry if the treat hadn't

stemmed from a row. If his mother hadn't said, 'He's your bloody child too, Lee, you deal with him for a bloody change,' in a weak voice which nevertheless travelled from her bedroom, downstairs, across the hall and into Kyle's ears as he perched on a kitchen stool hoping someone might come and make breakfast.

His mother called to him then, 'Kye, babe, come for a hug, Big Fella,' so he took off his school shoes in case they soiled the carpet and went upstairs. She was still in bed, in the room she now shared not with his dad, but with their Easter surprise, baby Jay. 'Relegation, son,' his dad told him with a joyless wink. She hadn't hugged Kyle once since Jay's arrival. Wanting her to felt like a fist in the soft spot where his ribcage parted, where boys at school do Heimlich manoeuvres on you for a laugh. But he wanted the mother she once was, the one with a flat belly and navel jewel, who fixed pancakes exclusively for him. He couldn't go near this whale with grey patches on her T-shirt where the milk leaked from her patties. He stayed in the doorway, said, 'Bye,' and fled.

The cars ahead inched forward and stopped again. Kyle's dad said, 'Sod this for a game of soldiers,' and pulled the lorry into a side street that led downhill. Soon they were whizzing along the lane that ran the length of the vale, trees arching overhead. Kyle's dad wound the window down and the roar was not traffic but the Ouseburn river handling last night's heavy rain.

After a while Kyle asked, 'Can you get to school from this way?' and his dad looked at him as though he'd never seen Kyle before in his life.

There were dustbins in the road outside the house of the deceased, put there by the two remaining Raymond sisters to save a parking space. Kyle's dad tooted as they turned into the street. The sisters, standing by the gate, looked up and waved, then seeing he wasn't slowing down, scrambled off the kerb to lug the bins back onto the pavement. He swung the lorry in beside them, so close he got their nerves going, got them laughing, even though their next of kin had died.

When he jumped from the cab, Kyle followed him, accidentally placing his palm on the horn, sending the sisters bolting and laughing again. Like father like son. His dad glared as he reached to lift him down. For a moment Kyle had those powerful arms, that beefy smell, all to himself before his dad set him on the pavement.

One sister, Winnie, stooped to Kyle and joked, 'Are you Mr Tosher of Tosher's House Clearance? Is that your assistant, eh?' Her face was orange with grey stripes where the powder had skipped the lines around her eyes and mouth.

'That'll be the day,' his dad said, unlocking the rear door and lowering the ramp.

'We got cartons for auction sellables,' Kyle told Winnie Raymond, 'bin bags for the dump and you yourself provide containers for keepsakes.' He'd often heard his father say so on the phone.

'Well-trained lad you have here,' Winnie said and Kyle's dad nodded graciously and smiled but didn't look at Kyle.

'Keepsakes?' asked the other sister. She was mauve from her set hair and veined cheeks to the sheen on her dress. The colour made her look more mournful than Winnie. She stepped forward and took Kyle's hand in hers, fingernails thick as horn.

'I'm Gertie,' she said. 'You'll have sharp eyes. I want you to find me something.'

'We've not got space for much,' Winnie started. 'We've all we want. The Lord's been very—'

'My sister had a locket,' Gertie butted in. Her watery eyes met Kyle's. 'A cameo locket of a girl dancing with skirts flying. I'll have that.'

'Yes,' said Winnie. 'That, we would like back. It was our mother's.'

Cameo. Locket. Kyle nodded, clueless. 'I'll keep me eyes peeled,' he said, hoping that would do.

His dad was beside them now, rod-backed and bowing stiffly as he took the sisters' hands. 'Don't worry yourselves about a thing. Whatever you're after we'll set aside, and letters and photos and whatnot. We know the biz.'

'It's just the locket,' said Gertie. 'Worth nowt but to us. I told the lad.' She squeezed Kyle's shoulder and beamed. Her teeth were the sort that come out.

'That's what we're here for,' said Kyle's dad, pulling a fiver from his back pocket, so crisp it looked like he'd ironed it. He lowered his head respectfully. 'Get yourselves off to The Bell, ladies. Have one on me in memory of a very fine woman.' There were tears in the eyes all round.

Inside was dark and smelled of soup. The deceased's last meal. The thought made Kyle's stomach turn. He stuck his nose in a pot of lilies on the hall console, but they were plastic and smelled of soup too, and of dust. His dad propped the front door open and they spent an energetic ten minutes chucking boxes down from the van and carting them inside. Then his dad opened the door to the lounge.

A high bed was jammed against the window where a sofa should be. This was where she died. Kyle had been past this house before, on his way back from football with mates, and had seen her sometimes at the window, rattling her lonely knuckles on the pane, beckoning them in. For a moment now she was back, stretched out on the candle-wick bedspread, dark goo flooding from her lips and eyes. *Melancholics* were cold, dry-skinned and spewed black bile.

'Get in here,' his father told him. 'You're neither use nor ornament standing there.'

She'd died in there. Kyle's eyes wouldn't move from the bed. Kitty Raymond moaned and rolled over. Her arms opened at him like his mother calling out for a hug, Big Fella. He gasped.

His dad stared at him. His face gave nothing away. Then he turned abruptly to a broad grey piece of appa-ratus by the bed. It looked like a pulpit on wheels. He kick started it and rode it across the room, grinning like a maniac.

'Know what this is?'

Kyle shook his head.

'A commode. A kharsi. Couldn't even make it to the proper bog.' He picked up an empty carton and tossed it through the air to Kyle.

'Don't join the freak show, Kylie. Clear the cabinet.'

Kyle hated when his father called him that. He edged into the room. The carpet was tacky underfoot. He opened a drawer. It was chock with medicine bottles, yellowing letters and the twisted remains of old support stockings. He didn't know where to start. In the glass-fronted cabinet top were ornaments. He opened it, lifted free a china greyhound.

'Where's the tissue?' he asked. His mum wrapped the Christmas ornaments each year. He knew that much.

'Eh?' said his dad. 'The Raymonds aren't the bloody queen. Pay peanuts, get monkeys.' He crossed to Kyle, yanked a drawer out of its socket, tipping the contents straight into a box.

'Get the picture?'

Kyle nodded.

'Make a start upstairs then.'

From the empty bedroom above, he could see the yard of his old infant school. The children were out, charging and shrieking. It had to be dinnertime already. His packed lunch was locked up in the lorry cab. If he were at school he'd have eaten it by now. Mrs Kendrick would be asking them to please put their fruit waste in a separate pile as it could make fine soil. Mrs Kendrick was of the light and airy Humour '*Sanguine*', though he'd never seen her bleed.

His fingers picked at the flaking paint of the radiator under the window. He got a good run on it, peeling one strip right over the top of the radiator and down the back. It was tricky to reach. His fingers felt the way, brushing off the thick fur of dust, which was human skin, Kitty Raymond's very previous skin, since she'd been downstairs for at least a year. The run of paint broke up and he lifted it free, feeling something grainy against his hand as he pulled it out. There, caught in the paint, was a fine gold chain, and hanging from it, dust choked, was a brown oval. He blew on it. The dust wouldn't clear. He rubbed it. A tiny white figure emerged. A slender, ladylike figure, like his mother before baby Jay arrived, dancing, skirts flying.

'I've found it! Dad, Dad, I've found it.' His legs were weak as he jumped the stairs three at a time.

His dad was not in the lounge. There were rustling sounds down the hall. Perhaps he'd started on the back rooms already. In the kitchen, the larder door was ajar. His dad stood inside, a bin bag open at his feet. He was eating Jammy Dodgers from Kitty's biscuit barrel. When he saw Kyle he poked the packet at him: 'You hungry, son? There's these or Breakaways.'

'I found the camion thing they were after. The thing they said. A locket, isn't it? Look, I found it.'

He handed the cameo to his dad. His dad held it high between his fingers. A thin shaft of light worked into the larder from the metal grille over the window. Dust swam in the air. The gold shone dully.

'That's it isn't it?'

His dad didn't look at it. He looked at Kyle.

'Yeah?' he said. He opened his fingers, let the cameo fall among the stale cereal boxes inside the rubbish bag.

Kyle felt a tilting sensation like the hunger in his stomach but lower down and more thrilling. His fist dug into his groin to keep the sensation alive. He wanted to see it again; his father's hands making waste of their promise to the Raymonds. He reached past his dad for a Breakaway. Its wrapper was stuck to the shelf and he cocked his head in disgust.

On the way home his dad wound the windows down again because the back reeked of Kitty Raymond's clobber. In Kyle's pocket was a twenty-pound note the sisters had given him for doing his best.

Life Pirates

O N   E A S T E R   D A Y afternoon, bright as glass, Ted
and I took Claude out for a walk. In the park she
found her thumb for the first time, plugging it in past the
second knuckle and suckling strongly. We were peering
over the pram, marvelling at this advance and didn't see
the man on the bench till he shouted, 'Oi, you!' at me
and lunged towards us. Ted's instinct was for Claude not
me, thank God. He wheeled her away, leaving the man
on me, his head locked over my shoulder, his breath at
my throat.

'Want sommat to make you smile?' the man said. He
steered me across the grass so I couldn't turn to see where
Ted had taken Claude. His knees nudged against the backs
of my thighs, keeping me moving until we reached a bed
of primulas and pansies. There, protected by the thick
yew behind it, was what looked like a twig someone had
plunged into the ground. I recognised it straightaway. He
gripped my neck and pushed it down.

'Its got buds.' He pointed to slits of bright green on
the spindly branches. 'See? Sickliest little fucker you could
find. It's got buds.'

Then I heard Ted's voice coming closer: 'Off. Off her!'
Like he was ordering a dog. The man loosed his grip on
me enough to let me turn. Ted was alone.

'Where's Claude?' I could hardly get her name out.

'She's fine.'

Ted was on the man now, flicking that weightless runt of a drunk off me as though he were a bit of lint, tossing him into the flowerbed where he lay grinning up at me, pansies in his hair. I noticed he'd lost a tooth at the side since I'd seen him last.

'Where's Claude?' I asked again.

'I bumped into Jenny. They're over there.'

We backed away. Ted's shoulders were up around his ears. 'Next time it could be Claude.' He paused, then said, 'Are you all right?'

'I'm fine. I wasn't afraid. He didn't harm me.'

'What did he say?'

'He, er, wanted to show me his shrub.'

'Is that a euphemism?' He sounded relieved I was taking the episode lightly. No need to burden himself with concern for me. One person is enough for anyone to care about wholeheartedly and these days he had Claude.

Jenny was heading for us, wheeling Claude briskly, her face all anxious. Ted broke into a trot towards them. I stole a glance back at the man. He was up on his feet again, tottering around the flowerbeds. He stuck a thumb up at me, touching himself through his jeans with the other hand. Then Jenny was embracing me and Claude was put into my arms, eyes closed now, still guzzling her thumb.

I heard Ted telling Jenny, 'She's OK. He's just a drunk.'

He wasn't though. He was Davy Shots, tragic local weasel, who wore a coat handed down from his dad, no matter the weather, a hounds-tooth check that reached the ground. Its pockets sagged with the bottles of moon-shine wrapped up in wallpaper that earned him his name.

We met on a high cliff. All cliffs are high but this was higher than the one on the other side of the ravine. Its path had collapsed. It offered more places where a girl might lose her footing and tumble into the screaming water far below. That's why I walked there. Davy walked behind me. I knew someone was following me but in those days I had no desires, so I wasn't afraid. You can't have fear without desire. The two are always balanced. The more store you set by your happiness the more frightened you can afford to be. The flip side of not caring is it makes you invincible and I wanted to be vincible. Vinced. Vinced to shreds.

I heard a branch snap and turned. He stood there, half a twig in each hand, broken on purpose to alert me to his presence. He saw me take this in and winked. I sat down on a rock that overhung the edge of the ravine to show I didn't give a toss that he was there—he didn't scare me. Davy came and sat so close his thigh pushed against mine, and asked me for a cigarette. I swapped one for a light. The cold came up at us from the rock, straight through our flesh, heading for bone as we sat and smoked. Davy told me his coat was warm and had once been his dad's. He lifted one side of it and wrapped it over me like a wing.

I had seen him in the streets and avoided passing too close, his mouth always working its way through silent obscenities and furious questions. I'd assumed the coat reeked. Close up it smelled of damp wool and cigarettes and spirits, but the satin lining smelled simply of Davy, not strong or sour but clear and distinct, like a plain voice sustaining a note.

'I've been following you,' he said, his thigh against mine so hard it slid me across the rock, nearer to the edge. 'You're going to jump.'

I just looked at my cigarette, how the heat crawled up the paper and spent it. I had almost no thoughts in those days, so I had the space to notice paper turning to ash. It wasn't a metaphor or a threat to my money or health, it was just a quiet, slow burn. I drew on the cigarette still watching its end burn now brighter and faster as I sucked.

Davy's head was touching mine. His hair smelled faintly woody.

'What's stopping you?'

I shrugged. 'The letters to people who should know.'

'Aye, the letters are a bugger.' He pulled his bottle from his pocket. 'How long do you reckon to get them right? Couple of days? A week?' He swigged and passed the bottle to me. A sweet flavour from Davy's mouth reached my lips before the taste of the moonshine. His question seemed to be heading for another. I wondered if he was after my possessions to flog at a boot sale.

'Is there stuff you want Davy?'

He jumped back in stagey amazement.

'You know my name!'

'These bring notoriety.' I touched the bottle and the coat.

'There's me thinking you had your eye on me.'

The idea of sozzled little Davy being an object of my desire.

'If there's anything of mine you want, take it. I'll give you a key.'

'Can I have a fuck?'

I thought I'd misheard.

He put his hand on my knee and squeezed. 'What's it to you? You're shrugging off this mortal coil.' He peered round at me, trying to force eye contact. I kept my head down.

'I'm right, aren't I?' He tightened his grip, digging his fingers into my knee, releasing his grip then digging again, to let me know it was intentional.

'Feel that?'

His thumb found a nerve and pressed, sending flashes of pain right up to my skull.

'Yes, I can feel that.'

'Feel something, then,' he said, satisfied, and let go.

He walked me away from the ravine and up to Hopkins House where I worked as sole skeleton staff in the winter months, writing leaflets about forthcoming events and dusting Hopkins's alleged desk and bed. It's a tiny museum in a house where the poet Gerard Manley Hopkins apparently once stayed for a week or so and is purported to have written the first draft of some devotional poems. It's funded entirely through a trust left by a dowager of the nearby Catholic church. They refuse to advertise on the net. We don't get many visitors.

'So, you work here,' he said. He looked impressed. 'I came to these parts in honour of Hopkins.'

That surprised me, just as he meant it to.

'More fool you,' I said. 'It's dubious he ever stayed here.'

Davy cocked one skinny leg up on a flower pot by the step of the house and thumped his chest:

I am gall, I am heartburn. God's most deep decree
Bitter would have me taste: my taste was me.

'Your inner Jesuit shines through,' I said.

He winked at me again.

'Ta,' he said.

As we parted, Davy said courteously, 'If you ever want that seeing to, do get in touch,' and fished in his pocket, handing me a card. When he was a few yards off from me he threw both hands in the air, one still holding his bottle, and did a little Fagin dance, like the Davy he'd been when I avoided him in the street. His card was smudged and frayed at the corners. It read:

David McClean
Life Pirate
Odd jobs taken
4c, Maudsley House, Copstall, Lancs——pl. call in person.
07770 4099495

It was February then, hardly the month to change your mind about hanging in there. Davy appeared at my workplace a few days later. We'd left it non-committal after the cigarette-knee thing. He showed no sign of our ever having met. He was after some work.

'I do odd jobs,' he told me. 'Shirley, that use to be the curator, she had me do the windows this time of year. I clear the guttering while I'm at it.' There was beer on his breath and he looked primed for a battle. He must have encountered some jobsworths since Shirley.

'Be my guest,' I said.

'Aren't you going to ask my fee?' His eyes worked the room. I couldn't tell if he was wavering over spiking the price up or bringing it down. 'It's thirty quid, all in.'

I was in Hopkins' study. Last summer some git had scored his desk with a key or a ring. I'd repaired it but it was showing up again now. I dipped the cloth in walnut oil and rubbed. I liked the smell, and how the pale yellow scratch darkened and disappeared as the oil sank in. But you can't stay around on the basis of that. Late in the afternoon I heard a clanging and the squeak of chamois leather across glass. I went round the back of the desk and polished the part no one sees. When I looked up, a ladder was leaned against the window outside and Davy's small feet in worn baseball boots were half way up it. The window frame cut him off at the hips, reminding me of his offer.

By the time I left work it was dark outside. I nearly tripped over him on the porch steps.

'About time,' he said. 'I'm freezing my nuts off here. How's those letters coming on?'

When we reached the end of the drive he turned right, in the direction of the ravine. It was slippery with half-rotted leaves. Davy took my hand. His was hot and urgent, tugging me down the unlit path like a child.

'I can't see,' I said.

'So fucking what? Thought you wanted to fall.'

The ravine roared at our side, breathing up wisps of mist against our faces. He stumbled and I pulled him up. I stumbled and he fell on top of me. I thought he might take this opportunity for a spot of assault, but he righted himself and we sat where we'd landed. He lit a cigarette, his hand cupping the flame so well it gave out no light. We passed his moonshine to and fro until my head felt fired up and detached from my body like a barrage balloon.

'What's it to be?' he asked. 'You going to shag old uncle Davey now or tell me what tipped you?'

I told him about the baby. About finding out I'd lost it on an outing to Dungeness when I was three months pregnant. How crudely, brutally symbolic the whole day had been, with a storm brewing and the soles of my feet so tender it felt like walking on knives as we trailed round Derek Jarman's garden, admiring piles of desolate stones in charred driftwood cages. How it ended with a tiny knot of blood in my pants at the miniature railway by the black and landlocked lighthouse overlooking the nuclear power station.

'When was this?' Davy asked. His coat was around me, his voice was as I'd never heard it: soft.

'Last June.'

I saw the lit cigarette-end bounce as he counted on his fingers.

'You were due this month.'

'Yes.'

'Due date?'

'Seventeenth.'

Davy caught me snorting and said, 'What?'

'Nothing. 'Due date.' Sounds funny coming from you.'

'Why?' asked Davy. 'I've got seven kids, me.' He snorted back and pulled on the cigarette. 'They all live with their mothers.'

The seventeenth was a Sunday. We met by the gates to Hopkins House. It felt like a date. Half way along the collapsing path I felt a hot flood of blood between my legs, soaking my jeans right down to the ankles. The side of the ravine reared up at me and I skidded. Davy caught me, took off his coat and put it round me. He wore a black shirt underneath and black jeans; he looked slender and surprisingly well.

By the time we reached town, my legs felt like sponges. I found the shot bottle in his coat pocket, pulled it out and drank from it. People tutted and glowered and crossed pavements. One woman even blinkered her child's eyes with her hands. I thought how restrained Davy was, after all, not to sneer and roar back at them more than he already did. Just when I wasn't sure I could last the final mile to my flat, he grabbed me and slid his hand inside the coat, past my breast to the pocket and pulled out his key.

'Dump, sweet dump,' he said.

So on the day that my baby should have been born, I was in Davy Shot's freezing bathroom with rust stains under the taps and mould between the tiles, having a bath. As soon as I got in, the water filled up with blood.

'Holy shit,' Davy said, walking in on me. He thought I'd found his razor. He leaned in to pull the plug and the red water drained away, leaving me naked in front of him. I found I wasn't embarrassed. He'd sussed more about me than my body could ever reveal. He rested his hand on my shoulder to balance himself as he put the plug back in and ran a fresh bath. Only then did he seem to notice I was naked and wet and he was touching my skin. His fingers rubbed my shoulder slowly, then up into my hair. He stood up.

'Ready for me?'

I stared at him. I still felt nothing at all. I nodded. He unbuttoned his shirt and spread it wide. I stared. All over his body, his skin was distinctly piebald brown and white. He pulled off his jeans. His legs were deeply dappled. An island of white skin illuminated his groin. He moved towards me. His cock was white with a neat stripe of brown curling round it like a candy. He wasn't aroused.

'Budge up,' he said. 'This is all my hot water till Monday.'

When I share baths with Ted I move forward to the tap end, but I slid back and let Davy in front of me. I wanted to see. His back was a map of white and brown islands and seas. I read once, when you're in despair, find one small thing you like of your own accord, not because anyone has taught you to like it or directed you to it. One thing, and concentrate on that. I scooped up water and splashed it onto Davy's back. He wriggled. The blood was diluted in this second bath. The water was rose tinted.

I went to bed for a week. When I was back on my feet I went into work. Davey didn't show up for any more odd jobs and I didn't call by his flat to find out where he was.

I'm not sure I could have found it, anyway. But I did hear from him one more time.

The first day I was up I felt shrouded from the world, the way you do by a heavy cold—my senses had all cut out. Ted and I were arguing. I wanted to plant a tree in memory of the baby. I'd decided it had to be a rare yellow maple. Ted said I'd picked the weakest variety of that species. I didn't care. He phoned around the garden centres and reported back to me that no one stocked it. One nursery owned up to a single ailing specimen, but they said it wouldn't thrive in this part of the country. I could hear Ted concurring with them. He put down the phone and it rang immediately. He picked up, listened and frowned.

'Collect call from Hopkins House. Will you accept the charges?'

'I always accept the charges,' I told him. And to Davy Shots I said: 'No I can't. Because I'm having a row with my husband about planting a tree in honour of our dead baby.'

Ted winced. He thought I was talking to the Chair of the Hopkins House Trust.

'I want an *Acer palmatum shirasawanum* but there's only one in the whole county and it's already so dead the nursery won't even sell it to us because they said we'd only ask for our body back. I mean our money back.'

'Nick it,' said Davy Shots.

Claude was awake. Her hands reached for my hair and tugged hard.

'Ouch, Claude.' I tried to untangle myself, but her fingers were so delicate and my hair so tightly caught in them.

'We're too passive,' Jenny was saying. 'A man assaults you and you just let it pass. It's not OK.'

'I'm fine,' I said. 'I think I know him anyway. He hangs around the museum. Claims he's a Hopkins' scholar.'

'Really?' said Ted. 'Why do I have my profound doubts?'

When we came to a fork in the paths, I took the low one that led past the bench Davy had returned to. I split from our group and went up to him, taking Claude with me. I meant to thank him for the tree, but he lifted his arm over his eyes and hollered, 'Keep that bairn away from me. I've eight of me own.' The sound startled Claude and she began to cry. I backed away. Jenny and Ted were shaking their heads. It was too cold to stop, so I unbuttoned my coat and latched Claude on as we walked, feeling the strong pull of her thirst right through my body.

We headed back past the spring bedding plants. Now that Davey had pointed it out to me, I could just make out the tiny *Acer shirasawanum* behind them, its new buds rising from grey wood like dots of light.

Ted had rung round all the nurseries to find it. Davy, phoneless, must have done the same on foot. He'd tracked down the specimen Ted had insisted we reject, and he'd nicked it. He'd remembered its long Latin name. Last February he must have brought it here and planted it.

Leave comfort root-room, Hopkins wrote, begging himself to forgive his own misery. I imagined the maple being smuggled out of its condemnatory nursery under one wing of Davy's hounds-tooth. I imagined that its sap, sensing and trusting the clear, plain air inside the coat, had sent messages through the body of the tree, to change its heart right then about withering and allow itself to take root.

Acknowledgements

'The Paperback MacBeth' was commended in the Society of Authors' Olive Cook Award and first appeared with 'Beau de L'Air' in the anthology *Even The Ants Have Names,* published by Diamond Twig Press; 'Mango' and 'The Last Of Her' first appeared in *The New Writer;* 'Ultimate Satisfaction Everyday' appeared as in the London stories anthology *33 East,* published by Glasshouse Books; 'The Dust Volcano' was a Commonwealth Prize winner and broadcast on the BBC World Service; 'Moleman' was online at *Pequin* ezine; 'Dog In The Yard' was anthologised in *Pleasure Vessels,* a collection of Ian St James Award stories published by Angela Royal; 'Life Pirates' came out in *The Yellow Room Vol 4* and 'Guava Heads' is forthcoming in issue 5. 'Mudlarks' is forthcoming in *The New Writer.* 'The Tenth Mother' was in *QWF Vol 35;* 'Things Like Meat' in *Brittle Star Vol 2;* 'Odissi Dancing' in *World Wide Writers Vol.11.*

Many thanks are due to Margot Stedman, Tania Hershman and Elaine Chiew for their invaluable feedback on the selected stories; to writers at The Round Table; Alison Fell's and Michelle Lovric's writing groups and the original Brittle Star writers for their critical insights over the years. Above all, thank you to Simon Cherry for his support, wit and inspiration along the way.

SUSANNAH RICKARDS comes from Newcastle-upon-Tyne and now lives near London. Her prose and poetry have appeared in UK anthologies and literary magazines, have won or placed in awards including Commonwealth, International PEN, Society of Authors' Olive Cook Award, The Ian St James, BBC Opening Lines, Crime Writers' Association Debut Dagger, Conan Doyle, and Fish. She's been the recipient of an Eastside Bursary and a Hawthornden Fellowship in Writing, was Writer-in-Residence at Middlesex University for two years and now teaches creative writing locally. Her first novel was short-listed for the Cinnamon New Novel Award. She has twin sons.